05 Dec 21

Praise 1

D0468991

"Reading *This Quiet Sky* ⟨ ⟩ *of Green Gables* with its elegant sense of nostalgic charm before it tragically and beautifully collides with the mysteries of life…Tucker's and Sarah's story is definitely not a tale to miss; it's the story of a first kind of love not easily forgotten."
—Rissi Cain, INSPY Award advisory board member

"Heartbreakingly romantic and absolutely poignant, Joanne Bischof has written a story that will captivate readers and leave an indelible mark, long after the last page is turned. I couldn't put this one down!" *—Katie Ganshert, award-winning author of A Broken Kind of Beautiful*

"Bischof's ability to create a complete storyworld in my mind never fails to impress, and Tucker and Sarah's love story will be part of me now. A standout young adult read…" *—Heather Day Gilbert, author of God's Daughter*

"In *This Quiet Sky* Joanne Bischof delicately balances a tender story of friendship and young love woven with threads of *what-if*. Bischof's writing rings true – equal parts the reality of possible loss that is overpowered by hope and the choice to love above all else." *—Beth K. Vogt, author of Somebody Like You*

"Joanne Bischof connects with readers [with] emotions that are both raw and endearing, and authenticity that grips your heart. I was deeply moved, and walked away from this story with Sarah and Tucker's journey firmly rooted in my heart..." —*Kristy Cambron, author of The Butterfly and the Violin*

"A must read for teens and adults, *This Quiet Sky* is a gentle reminder of God's unchanging love." —*Karen Cecil Smith, author of Orlean Puckett: The Life of a Mountain Midwife*

Praise for the Cadence of Grace series

"A gem by an author sure to draw fans." —*Publishers Weekly*

"Joanne has hit a home run with her Cadence of Grace series...this is the kind of story that will have readers telling their friends, 'You've got to read these books.'" —*Lauraine Snelling, author of the Red River of the North series*

"A tender story, told with loving care..." —*Liz Curtis Higgs, New York Times best-selling author of Mine Is the Night*

"Joanne has the rare talent of creating such compelling characters and story worlds that I wish her books would never end." —*Serena B. Miller, RITA Award–winning author of The Measure of Katie Calloway*

This Quiet Sky

a novella

JOANNE BISCHOF

This Quiet Sky

By Joanne Bischof

ISBN-13: 978-1502340030

ISBN-10: 1502340038

ALSO BY JOANNE BISCHOF

Be Still My Soul

Though My Heart is Torn

My Hope is Found

JOANNE BISCHOF

"Promise me you'll always remember:
You're braver than you believe, and stronger
than you seem, and smarter than you think."
— A. A. Milne

Christopher Robin to Winnie-the-Pooh

This Quiet Sky

By Joanne Bischof

Was that your first day in school there?

Yes.

Why did they seat you next to him?

I didn't have my own books and we were the same grade.

I certainly hope you didn't get too acquainted.

Why do you say that?

Well, you knew he didn't have long to live, didn't you?

I'd heard.

Seems that was terribly unfair to place you next to him.

Are you all right, my dear?

…I'm fine.

ONE

Rocky Knob, Virginia
1885

He has the kind of face that girls whisper about. Except there's something deeper there and I feel a twinge of sorrow. That feeling when something lovely is about to be spent. Wasted. I'm staring straight into this face as the teacher—Mr. Davis—leads me down the aisle to the back of the one-room schoolhouse and points to the bench beside the boy with the furrowed brow.

"This is Tucker O'Shay," Mr. Davis says. "You two will be using most of the same books, so I'll sit you together for the time being. Since you mentioned your low marks in mathematics, Sarah, we'll do an assessment for that today."

The young man—Tucker—looks up at me again. Mr. Davis marches back the way he came as a trio of young students walk in late—cheeks rosy from what was no doubt a bit of a run.

With nothing in hand but a clammy grip of calico skirt, I sit and drop my attention to the desk. This is the student. The seventeen-year-old boy the neighbor girls warned me about on the mile-long walk to school this morning. They took no care to hide their fascination over his fatal illness, all the while teasing that whatever he has is catching and since neither he nor I stayed behind to work our farms or get hitched to someone, we'd be the only students in the upper class and I would likely sit next to him.

I try not to take any of their teasing personally.

And decide that since this Tucker O'Shay is in school, he can't possibly be contagious.

The young man is slouching in his seat and doesn't appear to be doing anything productive. I've never known anyone facing their own end like this, so I peek at him and he's doing nothing more than turning a pencil in his fingers. I take quick inventory of his face again and for some strange reason, notice that the odd shape of his ears is surprisingly endearing. Jaw square, mouth full and shapely, skin pale. He's somewhat robust, not frail as I'd imagined, but his eyes are piercing...focused...and rimmed in shadows. He's looking around at anything but me. I *suppose* he could look like someone who's dying. But of what, I don't know, and I'm certainly not going to ask him.

Then he clears his throat and I realize that I'm staring.

Face suddenly aflame, I drop my gaze and focus on sitting very still. This doesn't last long. Mr. Davis tromps back and hands me a book labeled *Second Course in Algebra* along with instructions to answer all of the questions on page 149 to see where I'm at with mathematics. I positively hate algebra and barely scraped through the first course last year. This is going to be a disaster.

Peeking down the center aisle of the Rocky Knob schoolhouse, I see that my little sister, Betsy, has some kind of exam all her own. Our new dresses were cut from the same bolt of autumn-hued cloth, and her hair is loosely pulled back with a ribbon the same way mine is. Except her ribbon is green, where mine is black, and her hair is more than a few shades blonder than my muddy red. She looks back, crosses her eyes at me, and I smile as she faces forward. The teacher must have noticed.

He's a portly man with a scowl that looks etched into his face, and it just grew more pronounced. "Fifteen minutes, Miss Miller." His tone is laced with warning and I'm not sure if he's talking to her or me.

"Yes, sir," we answer in unison.

Some of the children snicker.

I don't know many of them. My family just moved here two weeks ago from South Carolina. We're poor as church mice, and though I'm convinced that our cabin will cave in if a crow lands on the stovepipe, it's now home. The Virginia mountains have their own kind of beauty, but I'm going to miss the sea.

Recalling that I'm being timed, I try to focus on the exam and read the first equation to myself. $49 = 3x + 8^2$. There are parentheses involved, and that bit rests atop a line with another x^2 just below.

What?

I stare at the problem and know that I need to make sense of this. It'd be a shame to be held back because of how I handle the next fifteen minutes of my life. I suppose that could be said for a lot of things.

Time to concentrate. I decide to square the eight and make it sixteen. Or should it be sixty-four? Indecision is trailed by a wince. Since sixteen came to mind first, I jot that down.

The boy beside me coughs into his fist.

I ignore him, and when he coughs again, I inch a little farther away on the seat we share. He's not dying *now*, is he?

Pay attention, Sarah. I draw a line through the first x and then the second. Perhaps they just cancel one another out. I'm guessing now, which has my palms sweating, so I set the chalk pencil down to wipe them on my skirt. The boy beside me coughs again and I brave a glance to make sure that he's not going to collapse in my direction. At the very least, I could move out of the way first.

He steals a little look at me and his blue eyes widen slightly—first at me, then down to my slate. Understanding comes. He's been looking at my arithmetic and this is what all the coughing is about. I place my elbow on the desk, fold up my arm, and prop the side of my head in my hand using my hair as a shield when it slips to the desk between us. Grabbing up the slate pencil, I stare at my work then discreetly erase the sixteen and turn it into sixty-four. I'm certain this is correct, so when he coughs again, I glare at him through a gap in my hair.

His brows shift upward—a look that suggests he's feeling quite justified in his nosiness and somehow confirms that I have every number wrong on the slate.

Pretty sure this constitutes as cheating—and certain

cheating is a sin—I decide to pretend like he doesn't exist and jot down a sloppy *30* as my answer.

"For pity's sake!" he hisses in a whisper. "The answer is *two*."

I slam my slate pencil down with a crack. "Will you stop it!" I shout.

His eyes shoot wide. Mr. Davis, who had been speaking to a group of young pupils, falls silent. Both pieces of the broken slate pencil clink around on the floor at my feet until they still.

Next come the words that slice dread through me. "Is there a problem, Miss Miller?"

I swallow hard and peer up at the teacher who has turned away from the blackboard, chalk still poised from where he was about to begin writing.

"No, sir," I choke out weakly.

"Were you accustomed to performing such outbursts at your last school?"

My voice barely comes. "No…sir."

"Please come here. Bring the textbook."

The whole class has turned to stare, and my legs feel like soggy reeds as I stand. Tucker is looking up at me with a mixture of shock and amusement. I decide to harness any remaining dignity and ignore him.

At the front of the classroom, Mr. Davis takes the book from me and scrawls the first problem across the top of the blackboard. It's the one I was just struggling with, and when he finishes, he pounds the final x into place so hard a piece of chalk chips off. "You will solve this problem and the rest on the page in front of the class. Am I understood?"

Speechless, I can only nod.

"Miss Miller?"

I fight the dryness in my mouth to answer. "Yes, sir."

"Good."

How I wish my hand was steadier as I take the chalk from him. Starting on the far left of the blackboard, I begin. I place a few numbers here and there, then circle a *two* as the answer. At least I'll get this one right. Tucker O'Shay is probably wallowing in smugness right now.

Mr. Davis delves into a history lesson and the afternoon drags on like it's hitched to the back of a snail.

By the time I've written out and attempted to solve the next problem, I glance back briefly. Just long enough to see that the boy who got me here is leaning back in his seat. Staring at me as if he means to make the most of it. I glare at him before turning back around and manage to pour all my attention onto the third problem, barely finishing by the time noon rolls around and school is dismissed for the lunch hour. As students of all ages shuffle out the door, I glimpse my sister giving me a sorrowful look. It's surprisingly comforting, and determined to see this through to the noblest end I can muster, I give her a small smile.

I barely notice Tucker step out.

The sound of playing children fills the air. Mr. Davis eats his meal at his desk. His jaw clicks when he chews and he says nothing about me being excused, so I fight a sigh and begin the next problem.

The wall clock reads a little past three when I finally step outside the schoolhouse to find Betsy sitting on a round stump, chin in hand, waiting.

The late spring air hits me for the first time since that morning. Betsy is chattering away to a nearby squirrel. In fact, she may be singing. She's eleven, but is rather short, which makes it easy to forget that she's not a little girl. Her attention shifts to me, and as if knowing how hungry I am, she hands me one of the hard tea biscuits from the dinner pail. I accept it gratefully. Within moments she's talking on and on about the day as we step around the far corner of the schoolhouse.

It's a quaint little building that looks like it was whitewashed a few lifetimes ago. An oak stands tall beside it, drooping crooked limbs near some of the windows brushing young, green leaves against the glass in a charming way. Betsy and I amble through the open schoolyard and down the lane. It's a mile to home, and our neighbor girls, the Nettles, are gone. They had mentioned staying around and waiting for me, but with school being over at two o'clock, I told them to head on home while I finished. No sense in everyone being late to their chores because of me.

I try not to think about the utter embarrassment that just occurred over the last few hours. I fear I may have gotten many of the equations wrong and in front of the whole class to boot. Just grand.

We're in the woods now and old leaves are soggy underfoot with recent rains. This was our first day walking here, and without the neighbors' guidance, I'm hoping we don't get lost. Recalling having followed a narrow road, I glance around for that as we walk and have just spotted the curving lane in the distance when something else catches my eye. It's Tucker. He's leaning against a tree, looking at me with that furrow to his brows that hints at curiosity. It's mixed with the spark of amusement that reminds me how much I don't like him.

I look past him and walk on.

"Wait—"

I keep going, angling toward the ridge that will take us home, but have the horrid feeling he's following us. He is, slowly, which could be an act. Spotting a nearby tree branch, I bend and pick it up. It's heavy and awkward and I look ridiculous, but I will hit him with it if I need to defend my sister. He mutters something sarcastic that makes Betsy giggle and me pretty sure I should just toss the stick and forget any need for heroics. There's a scuffle of leaves and I glance back again to see he's started to jog a little. Then he winces.

"Please don't make me run." He's slowing to a walk again, holding his gut as if he's in pain.

And now I feel sorry for him. Drat. I slow to a halt, drop the stick as subtly as possible, and turn. He's smiling at me, which makes everything worse. His expression flinches again and he bunches his hand into a fist as if to keep from holding his side. I swallow hard.

"What do you want?" Maybe I'm not going to make

him run, but kindness is hard to muster.

"I want to talk to you. First of all, I'm awful sorry that you got in so much trouble. I didn't know you had such a temper, or I wouldn't have bothered you."

A little squeak slips out of my throat. Was that supposed to be an apology? He's lucky I dropped the branch.

Grabbing Betsy by the hand, I march on as fast as humanly possible. He falls behind within seconds.

"Sarah," he says softly.

I ignore him.

He gently calls my name once more, but there's not much hope in it and I can hear that he's farther back now. I speed onward toward the road, practically dragging Betsy, who's voicing little protests, so I slow a tad for her. I'm determined not to glance back, but with the silence peek to see that Tucker has his hand braced against the side of a tree and is trying to lower himself down to sit. He's having a hard time and looks to be in pain. Guilt hits me, so I let my hair fall across my shoulder in that shield again and turn my face away so I don't have to see.

I honestly think of taking another step toward home when Betsy tugs on my hand—in which direction—I don't know, but I slam my eyes closed and take a deep breath. What am I doing?

The air shoots out of me, replaced by a fresh determination, and I turn around. Seeing Tucker sitting on the ground, one knee pulled in, I suddenly forget how to be angry with him. I let go of Betsy's hand to start that way. "Are you all right?" I call softly.

Not looking at me, he nods.

"Can I...help you?"

He shakes his head, then squints up at me through one eye. "Just waiting a minute would be good enough."

I can wait a minute. It feels strange to be standing over him, so I kneel. The damp ground moistens my stockings and Betsy walks over a few paces to perch on a fallen log.

"Attempts of apology aside, I need to tell you something." He draws a slow breath and winces once more. "It's Mr. Davis..." His blue eyes find mine. "He asked me if I would tutor you in algebra. In the mornings."

All I can do is blink. A rush of reactions come and I don't know which one to accept. "Me?"

"Are you this bad with all mathematics?" A stubborn bit of his hair swoops up in the front and he gives it a tug as he says this.

"I know it isn't my strongest subject."

Despite the fact that he still seems in pain, he chuckles a little. "No. Not exactly." He looks over at me with an impish light in his eyes.

"You waited around to tell me?" I'm not sure what to make of this. "Mr. Davis didn't mention it."

"No. I told him I would."

Curious, I ask why.

"Well, for one," he shifts a little on the ground, pulling his other knee in, "so we could have this *lovely* chat in which you thought about beating me over the head with that stick."

I bite my bottom lip.

"And two, so I could tell you that I'm sorry. I really am sorry. I shouldn't have pestered you during your exam. You were just so terrible at it, I couldn't help myself."

Stiff, I change positions a little. "You're not very good at apologies."

"And you're not very good at algebra."

From her perch, Betsy chimes in. "That means you have somethin' in common."

I give her a little look and Tucker is smiling again. Then, as if realizing he's still sitting, he sighs—looking a tad embarrassed—and says something about needing to get home. He stands with more strength than I anticipate. With a "see you soon," he flashes a wink in my direction. But his gait is slow as he starts for home. With my thoughts already pinned to tomorrow, I take Betsy's hand again and do the same.

TWO

Mornings here are much like they were at my old school.

Everyone has a chore, and by pitching in, the schoolhouse stays clean and tidy. A boy who looks about thirteen polishes the blackboard while I sweep under the desks. Some of the younger girls open the windows. Their braids hang down their backs, little free curls hinting at the rain in the air from the night before. I've learned a few of their names. Little Dora has dark eyes and a spunky smile, while Clara doesn't talk much and is so thin I want to feed her what's in my dinner pail. They make friends with Betsy easily.

Two older girls bustle in and sit in the back row on the other side of the aisle from me. They look like they are sisters, perhaps fourteen and fifteen. They seem shy and keep to themselves, which is probably why I didn't really notice them over there the day before.

At eight o'clock, Mr. Davis calls everyone to order and we take our seats, lower grades in the front, older students in the back.

I keep to the right side of the bench I was assigned to, trying to ignore how the left side is empty. Mr. Davis writes *Friday, May 18th* across the top of the blackboard in his dark, crisp script, then turns and begins attendance. I raise my hand when he says my name. He doesn't call for Tucker. Just glances toward the back row and makes a mark in his book.

Arithmetic lessons begin for the little ones and I remember that this time is designated for algebra. There's not much I can do alone, so I peer out the window. My reflection peers back—a plain face atop an even plainer, oat-colored dress.

Though I combed and tied my hair over my shoulder with a gray ribbon today, it already looks untidy thanks to the dew in the warm air. Part of me wishes I could just wear it up in a soft, feminine bun as my older sister Maggie does, but I'm supposed to wait another year.

People always talk about how pretty Maggie is with her chestnut curls and dark, thick lashes. Sometimes they pay me the same compliment, but I think they're just being nice. My hair is the color of a dirty penny and I have freckles on my nose. I have no curves and am strong in a way that is very unladylike. Which is why I found my slate pencil in two pieces beneath the desk this morning.

The oak, with its branches of pointy, green leaves, bobs in greeting with the breeze, so I sketch some of it in a corner of my slate.

At nearly half past eight Tucker walks in.

His eyes go straight to me and it sends a twirling sensation through my stomach.

He has two books in his broad hand and sets them on our desk before sitting. He's breathing hard, but I can tell he's trying to be discreet about it. Mr. Davis says not a word about his late arrival. So…Tucker gets to waltz in whenever he wants. It must be his age. He *is* taller than Mr. Davis. Though the leniency could simply be an advantage to his condition. After what I saw yesterday, I doubt there are many.

The collar of his white shirt looks crisp and he's wearing a navy sweater pulled over it. Perhaps his mother knit it for him. Maybe an aunt or a grandmother. But the late May weather is quite fair. He must be cold. It hits me what that might mean, but before the thought even finishes, I notice again just how thoroughly handsome he is. Both realizations make me unhappy for very different reasons.

"You're staring at me again, Sarah Miller."

My face gets hot and I busy myself with aligning the slate in front of me while he settles in. "Good day, Tucker."

He sets a dinner pail at his feet. "Mr. Davis said we could spend the first two hours of school going over algebra."

"Two hours…"

There's a clatter beside us and something hits the ground. I look over to see that one of the older girls has dropped a metal pencil box. She leans over to gather up all that's spilled, but a short ruler has skidded to a stop beside Tucker's boot. Gripping the desk, it takes him a moment to pluck it up, and straightening, he hands it out to the girl with a friendly smile.

She looks at the ruler, then his hand. Finally to his face. Her eyes are wide.

I wait, uncertain as to what's going on. Then, tucking her hands into the folds of her skirt, she gives a small shake of her head, forcing a tight smile. Tucker nods a little. Some kind of resignation as he leans back against the seat. He does a playful little flip with the ruler—that seems to be covering up something deeper—before setting it on the edge of our desk.

He just sits there for a moment and I don't know

what to do or say. Was she afraid of touching something that he touched? Tucker's silence is piercing me as I search for words.

"Are you ready to begin?" he suddenly asks, looking sideways at me. There's a fierce layer of hope in his expression. "No going back. You'll never be able to be horrible at math again."

I find myself glancing at the ruler and something unsteady filters through me. As if I don't know what to do. But the feeling vanishes just as quick because I *do* know what to do. Which makes it easy to answer him. I tell him that I'm ready. No going back.

He smiles. His cool hand brushes mine as he takes control of my slate. "Now, I assure you that I'm a very good tutor. I'm also a whiz at algebra, so you're gonna be in tip-top shape in no time. Are you thinking of going to college?" The center of his brow rises as if that's a simple question. As if all girls just *go to college.*

"Me? Oh no." I'm not smart enough for college and my parents could never afford to send me. "No."

"What are you gonna do after this?"

"Uh…I suppose I'll get married. Have a family." That's what girls usually do.

"You seem very…marryable."

With his stab at encouragement, I can tell he's humoring me. "Thank you." My face feels hot again, so I redirect things. "What do you plan on doing?" I hope this isn't a bad thing to ask him. If his days *are* numbered, I don't know to what extent.

Stretching out a little, he resumes his slouching position, then glances up to where Mr. Davis is listening to a trio of students recite the multiplication table. "Well, I was planning on being the next president of the United States, but I'm not sure how that's gonna pan out." He tilts the top textbook toward me and begins searching for a particular page.

He seems to know what he's doing, and I brave a glance at his expression, hoping I didn't just offend him.

"We'll start with the basics." He takes my slate pencil, then scrawls a short equation of $x + 35 = 40$. His blue eyes lift to mine. "Can you tell me what x stands for?"

"Five?"

He smiles. "Yeah, five. But what will we be calling x?"

I have no idea. His smile deepens and I join him.

"X…is the variable. And we have two constants, thirty-five and forty. Does that make sense?"

I nod.

"So far so good."

The letters are the variables. I determine to remember this.

His arm brushes mine as he writes something new on the slate. "This one's going to be a little different." He scribbles *x + 23 = 2x + 45* and tries to make sense of it for me. We end up with *-22* as the answer.

Shifting, I kick a bit of skirt out of the way so I can adjust my foot in and lean toward the slate. This brings me closer to him, so I slide my arm across my lap. "I just don't understand the negative answer. It doesn't make sense."

He pulls a pencil from behind his ear. "No. It wouldn't."

"Why do you say that?"

"Because you're only lookin' at what's right in front of you. You did this yesterday."

"That's because the equations were—"

"No." He smiles and frees a folding knife from his pocket. "Not that. When you were walking home. The way you picked up the stick…like you were gonna hit me with it."

Can he not forget about that?

"You were going with the first thought that popped into your head again." Snapping the knife open, he presses it to his pencil and sharpens the tip with slow strokes from his thumb. "Same with when you answered all those questions wrong. You weren't considering the possibilities or the other angles. You just went with the first thing that made sense, and sometimes life doesn't work that way." Finished, he pockets the knife and looks at me. "Sometimes an entirely different equation than you expect is staring you in the face."

He's looking at me so intensely that I wonder if we're still talking about numbers.

Gently, he continues. "Maybe you should be a little more contingent in your thinking."

"Contingent?"

"I'm talking about the unexpected—"

"I know what it means." But I'm not sure what he's getting at, so I sigh and say, "All right. Explain."

"Thatta girl."

Freeing a notebook from his stack of texts, he dives into an explanation before he even finds a blank page. When he does, he begins forming equations. He talks on—describing the philosophy behind mathematics that doesn't entirely make sense, but he's so excited and thorough that I try and grasp it. Partway through, he pulls a piece of paper from his pocket and unfolds it. Scrawled everywhere are thoughts and more equations. Did he write this up last night? As he explains things, I realize that he must have when I see my name amongst the jumbles. I'm not sure what to make of that. The time he's spent on this. For me.

I'm suddenly wondering what his room looks like. Whether he has a desk. If it was there where he wrote my name sometime last night before he went to bed. This is a silly thought, but now I'm trying to think of him—his life. And what I'm immensely hoping are just rumors.

My gaze moves from the paper and books to his face. Those funny-shaped ears. I can't take it anymore. "Tucker?"

He's writing out an equation on my slate. "Yeah?"

"Are you…unwell?"

He blinks, then slowly finishes writing. Then he wets his lips and sets the slate pencil down. His nod is so brief, I almost miss it. "Yeah."

A sharpness expands in my chest that is very unpleasant. Like having to swallow something whole. "Very much so?"

Again, that small nod.

"May I ask…what's wrong?"

I realize he's shaking his head before I even finish. "Sorry, no." Spoken so firm and direct, there's no room for question. Then he leans the tiniest bit closer. A warm tingle tiptoes up my arm where his wool sweater brushes my sleeve. "But I can tell you that it's nothing catchable and you're perfectly safe."

To my surprise, I wasn't worried about that. A little pang hits my heart that he brought it up. I remember the way the neighbor girls joked about him. As if he was contagious. I glance around at the other students, none of which I've seen interact with him.

Does he not have friends?

Whatever I'd thought of him before, I now see only the shadows under his eyes and the way he's not quite looking at me. How his steps are somewhat slow. How he held his side yesterday, wincing in pain.

"I won't ask again," I say softly.

His voice matches mine, which is easy with us sitting so near. "Thank you."

I want to ask if it's truly incurable. But I can't…for his sake. And in a way, I just promised not to. "I hope you get better." Very much so.

A little light hits his eyes, going no further. "Thank

you."

But I feel like a child who's just been told that yes, Santa Claus is real. It's not the truth, and someday I'll find out what that truth actually is.

Somewhere in the distance, I hear Mr. Davis call on one of the older girls across the aisle who has her hand raised. Tucker and I ought to stay on task or we'll be in trouble. Tucker must have had a similar thought, for he plucks up the slate pencil and finishes the equation. He helps me solve it, then another, and another. I don't ask about him anymore and he doesn't ask about me, and it's best this way. We just focus on numbers and variables, and when the lunch hour comes, I thank him for his help and carry my pail out into the sunshine.

Within minutes, it's clear that Betsy is much more interested in playing tag than eating, so I settle in the shade of a tree by myself and pull out a piece of bread and one of the hardboiled eggs. Slow progress with peeling the shell gives me plenty of time to glance around. It's then that I spot Tucker sitting near the woodpile where the glow of noon brightens the grass. Leaning back against the sawn logs, he pokes at his food and glances my way. I look down, pick at my hardboiled egg and have to work to keep from looking up again. Everyone plays around him as if he's not there. Granted, he is seventeen and seems more like a man than a boy, but you'd think someone would at least say hello.

The thought of sitting by him comes and I try to push it away. It doesn't go so well. All I can think of is the way that girl wouldn't take her ruler back, and by the time I've finished my egg, I've decided that life is short. If I don't go now, I may never and I'll look back on this moment with regret. I stand, pick up my pail, straighten my skirt, and start that way.

Don't do this, Sarah.

Another few steps.

You're gonna regret this, Sarah.

But my heart's not listening and my feet are carrying me over to him. He looks up at me and stops chewing.

I set my pail beside his and settle down in the grass. "May I sit with you?"

Slowly, he starts chewing again, then swallows, still staring at me. "If you'd like."

I do. And also, "I want to thank you for your help this morning. I already feel that I've learned so much. L-Likely—" I stumble on the word when he seems amused by what I'm saying. "Likely we've only scratched the surface, but...whatever you teach me is an unexpected blessing." I smile and it's surprisingly easy. "How can I thank you?"

He looks a bit confused as he folds a napkin. That was a rather open-ended question.

I search for some way to fix that. "Do you like cookies?"

Still peering down, his expression is soft. "I do."

"Any particular kind?"

This draws his eyes to my face. "Nope. I like everything."

Then I will make him some for next week. It hits me that there's one in my pail today for Betsy and me to share. I can't remember what kind, so I pluck out the handkerchief and free a thick oatmeal cookie. I hold it out to him. "For putting up with me."

He smirks. "You're no trouble. You're actually very teachable."

"Teachable *and* marryable. Two compliments in one day?"

He laughs. It's a deep, sweet sound that makes me wish I had a brother just so I could hear that kind of laugh all the time. With me still holding out the cookie, he seems reluctant to accept it, so I place the round in his palm, and the brief brush of my skin against his shows he's a little warmer. I'm glad he's out here in the sun.

THREE

Roosters are kind of like mosquitos. You can swat at them but they don't go away. With the evening sun low in the sky, I give the rooster my best glare and skirt around him toward the nesting boxes in the chicken coop. All the while unable to forget about how he spurred Betsy yesterday, poor thing. After finding six brown, speckled eggs, I ease back by him, still glaring.

We're not friends, he and I.

After toting the eggs up to the kitchen, I slip back into the yard to help Betsy pin up laundry. She's too short for this chore really, but how I adore her for trying to help me in exchange for fetching the eggs. Chores on Saturday are a common occurrence in the Miller home. Once, when I was younger, I stitched a sampler that said *Wash on Monday, Iron on Tuesday, Mend on Wednesday, Churn on Thursday, Clean on Friday, Bake on Saturday*.

Why this is, I don't know. Ma never washes on Monday. She washes on whatever day of the week she wants, and last Thursday, while the churn sat collecting dust, Pa got so worried when she didn't appear around suppertime, he nearly went out to find her. Minutes later, we all spotted her hurrying across the meadow with a big smile and a pail of wild strawberries. Who needs butter when you can have those with cream for supper? Pa watched Ma across the table with a glowing face.

Beside me now, Betsy chatters on about the new friends she's made at school and how her first few days went. I'm glad that she's happy. Most of the children there are nearer to her in age and I can see that these hills are already feeling like home to her.

I don't know if that's possible for me, but I just listen and pin up a pair of Pa's denim overalls.

Ma and Maggie talk in the kitchen where they're shelling pecans. The nuts were a welcome gift from a neighbor, but I hate shelling pecans; I'd just as soon plop the sack back on the stranger's porch under the cover of night. Maggie's much more mild-mannered than I am, which is likely the reason why Ma shooed me out of doors today.

I listen to their chatter through the window as Betsy pins a damp apron on the line. Ma has a high, sweet voice. Maggie's is cool and smoky in a way that draws young men near her just to hear her say hello. She's telling Ma about such a one that she met at the post office in Mount Airy when she was there with Pa. In a soft voice, she mentions that he's nine years older than her. I don't catch his name and instead, hoist up the empty basket and motion for Betsy to follow me. In the cabin, Ma bends to press a kiss to Betsy's round cheek. Maggie, who finished school two years ago, pounds out a mound of dough and there's no more talk about men and post offices.

Thinking on my promise to make Tucker cookies, I discreetly ask to bake a batch to bring to school on Monday. Ma consents, though I know the ingredients will cost her. I make a vow to wash all the dishes tonight. With so much to do, the evening passes in a whirlwind. I usually hate dishwashing, but it's surprisingly no trouble tonight and Tucker's face keeps coming to mind. At nearly nine, the house smells like cinnamon and sugar when I find myself so tired that I fall asleep without saying my prayers.

I wake up early to remedy that and say an extra one for Tucker O'Shay.

Sundays are enjoyable here in Rocky Knob. The church is cozy with friendly people. As folks file in and find their places on the narrow, rough pews, I stride quietly behind Ma through the press of dark coats and try not to look around for a particular young man, but that seems to be all I can manage to do.

There's no point, really. He's not there.

He's also not at school on Monday. I set the tin of cookies on the bench beside me, thinking he may appear late, but the day trudges along and there is no Tucker.

Tuesday's the same.

By Wednesday, I've already given the cookies to my family and have prayed more times than I can count that Tucker's all right. I don't even know where he lives, or I might have gone by to discreetly check. I make it a point today to find this out. Mr. Davis may know. But I don't ask him when he brings me a book of spelling words to study, apologizing for Tucker's absences. Mr. Davis, who I now find hard to fully dislike, promises to carve out some time in the afternoon to go over a new lesson with me in algebra.

Disappointment settles deeper in my stomach.

A quick scan of the spelling book shows that I know most of the words already, so after a little while of repeating them to myself, I fold my arms and lower my forehead down. I spend the next few minutes mentally quizzing myself on the words, peeking at the book with each one to check if I'm correct. I have my head down, struggling to spell *Ecclesiastes*, when a voice is near my ear.

"So I was thinking…"

My head shoots up and I bite back a yelp. I look up at Tucker peering down at me. His eyes are wide as if I'm insane.

"Are you all right?" he asks, easing himself down.

My mouth opens to speak, but nothing comes. I clear my throat and force myself to appear normal. "You just startled me."

"Sorry 'bout that." With relaxed movements, he places his books on the desk between us, then slides me a glance that's so thorough, I wonder if he forgot what I looked like.

The disappointment has vanished. And now nothing is in my stomach but a bright, little flutter. It's a queer sensation. I rode a Ferris wheel once at the county fair near Charleston and it's the same…that feeling of leaving a part of you behind…way up high. It's a bit uneasy, but you don't want to change it for anything because it's worth it.

His brow does that quizzical little pinch and I realize I'm doing a poor job of appearing normal. He gives me a small smile and is still looking at me, but I know there's no possible way that he has that *way up high* feeling. I swallow hard, wishing I just didn't think to care. There's no reason to care. We're friends—it would seem—and I'm glad for that. It's nice to have a friend. I'm pretty sure we have this in common.

He's wearing that same blue pullover on top of his collared shirt. Then I notice that he's also wearing gray fingerless gloves and that he's not taking them off. Is he truly that cold? With summer near, the weather has been plenty warm. Tucker pulls a pencil from behind his ear and twirls it like a pinwheel with two fingers, around and around. "How's the student?"

"Very good." Yet now all I want to do is ask about the days he was absent. He probably doesn't want me to, so I simply say, "How are you?"

He smiles. "Very good. Do you have my cookies? I've been thinking of them all week."

I say that he forfeited them when he didn't come Monday or Tuesday.

"Sorry about that, too." He looks away and a little wall seems to nudge up between us. Then within moments, he's setting me up with a simple lesson. He wants me to answer some questions all on my own.

I work silently and he sits beside me, staring out the window.

Though I know you're supposed to be quiet in school, the silence feels strange after several minutes, so without lifting my eyes from my work, I whisper, "Why do you come to school if you don't seem to be learning anything?"

His body shifts—that detached demeanor fading. Leaning back against the seat, he folds his arms over his chest and peers at me. "Who says I'm not learning anything? And if I'm not mistaken, you were taking a nap when I walked in."

I roll my eyes. "I mean because you're the oldest boy in school."

Sitting forward, he plucks the slate pencil from my hand, causing his fingertips to brush mine. He erases the problem I've been attempting to solve, then rewrites the equation. "Do you mean that most fellas my age are all working with their pas? Or that some have taken on jobs at the lumber mill or the smithy or other places?"

I nod.

He slips the slate pencil back between my fingers and taps the slate—a silent but clear request to start again. "Some are even starting families of their own, I'd say."

He shrugs a little and seems uncomfortable. "But I suppose I'm not cut out for any of that."

My gaze slides to his face.

"So for now this keeps me busy. Gives me something to do aside from sitting at home with my ma worrying over me. I thought I'd take another year in school and then try my hand at the college entrance exams."

I shift to look at him. "Really?" The movement sends my ribbon slipping from my hair. "That's wonderful." I tug it free to re-tie.

"Thanks." Tucker's gaze follows my fingers for a moment. "Mr. Davis set it up. He has an old school chum who's a professor at Brown. They're going to let me take the exam in Danville where someone will meet me from the university. Pretty soon."

I smile at him. "I hope you do well."

He smiles back. "Speaking of which, I think you should try, too. Once we get a few more math skills into that pretty head of yours, that is."

Pulling the bow tight, I drop my hands. "There's no way I'm going to college. I'm not cut out for it. And truly, my family barely has the money for necessities." I tug a pinch of my faded dress to prove my point.

Twisting his mouth to the side, he doesn't say

anything else about it.

The rest of the day passes quickly. It's all business from there on out as we finish with algebra. Then, while I work on a literature essay, Mr. Davis calls Tucker to the front of the room. Books in hand, Tucker settles on a stool opposite the teacher at his desk and they talk amiably for a while. Soon after, Mr. Davis opens one of the texts and seems to begin an oral quiz of some kind.

After adding a few more sentences to my essay, I glance up to see that Mr. Davis has asked Tucker another question. Sitting straight on his stool, Tucker folds his hands behind his head, elbows jutted out straight. He squints his eyes closed tight, holding himself that way. I've never seen anyone think so hard. Finally, he answers. Mr. Davis looks puzzled and consults the open textbook, flipping back a few pages. Tucker leans toward him and points to something that sends Mr. Davis' eyebrows skyward.

There's something about the exchange that tells me Tucker is smarter than him.

Needing to finish my essay, I lose myself in words. The lunch hour comes, but I've fallen behind on time, so I stay in to finish. It's then that one of the little boys—a buck-toothed lad named Donald—tumbles from a tree he had climbed. He looks to be in one piece, but is holding his wrist and crying so fiercely Mr. Davis dismisses the class to scuttle the boy home.

I gather up my things, and when Betsy asks to go to the Nettles' house, I tell her to run along but to be home in time for supper or Ma will get worried. With a toothy grin, she dashes out the door with the neighbor girls.

Pail and slate in hand, I step out myself.

Tucker's there, leaning against the side of the schoolhouse. He straightens when I come down the steps. "May I walk you home?"

My heart shoots up. I look around to see if he could have been speaking to someone else. Knowing it's just me, I should stop hesitating, but the words don't come. He must take it for something else…

"I promise not to keel over."

I wince. "That's not funny."

He shifts his boots, and for the first time since I met him, he seems…nervous. I don't know why. "All right. I promise not to be morbid if you let me walk you home."

I stare at him. "You're bad at apologies *and* speaking to girls."

"And you're very good at insulting me." He tugs at the front of his hair. "Does this mean we're friends?"

I don't see anyone else around, so I guess we're stuck with each other. Moving down the steps to his side, I say as much and he gives me a lopsided grin.

FOUR

There's something about the way I step on and he joins me that feels right. He's a slow walker, so I make sure to match my pace to his as we follow the edge of a split rail fence that's bordering someone's farm. I don't want this to be any harder on him than it has to be.

We walk for a while and he eventually tugs his gloves off. He asks me about South Carolina and I answer all his questions and do my best to describe the sea near Charleston where we lived on Meeting Street. I ask him some of my own and learn that he's the youngest of three children and that his pa is an oat farmer. Tucker offers to hold my dinner pail, taking it easily. When I ask him about his quiz in school, he says it was on Latin and Greek.

So he truly is planning on going to college. I hate that this doesn't make sense. He has hopes for the future...but surrounding him is the fact that something's not right.

Aching for answers, I try to dig a little differently. "Do you really plan on being the president of the United States?"

"Absolutely. Somebody has to."

I've been watching the rutted path as we walk, so I peer up at him. "I hope it happens for you."

He smiles over at me, then his expression shifts slightly. "Do you still plan on being a housewife?"

"Um…I suppose."

"If you want it, say it with conviction, Sarah."

"Yes. I am eager and ready to become a housewife." But I'm actually not and he probably can tell, which is why he's teasing me.

"Much better. Though I think you could still use some practice." The breeze tousles his hair and he runs a hand forward through it. "You have conviction about certain things…" He speaks without looking at me. "They're just not the ones you acknowledge." When he finally does glance my way, his blue eyes filter across mine a few times. "You're so focused on being normal that you haven't realized that you're actually not."

I frown.

He smirks. "Don't worry, I mean that as a

compliment. That's one of the reasons why I like you."

Stunned, I laugh a little.

"And there are other reasons." He switches our dinner pails to his other hand and walks on as if he didn't just say that.

I'm waiting and I wish I wasn't, but he is going to finish that thought...isn't he?

Having had few opportunities, I've never been very comfortable with talking to boys. I just wet my lips and keep a gentle pace beside him.

"I like the way that you wear those ribbons in your hair." He halts, so I stop.

I feel my eyes go wide.

"And the color of your skin." He takes my arm and turns it gently in his fingers, shooting a thrill through my very core. "It's very pretty." He smiles as if that's an everyday kind of thing to say. "I like that you're terrible at math because I get to spend more time with you, and I like that you were thinking of hitting me with that branch. I can't even tell you how much I liked that." He starts chuckling as he walks on.

"You're not so normal yourself." But I can't get my feet to move. All his words hit my heart at odd angles, burrowing in, staying.

He slows, watching me, so I force myself to take steps. The woods are all around us now with their soft sounds and colors. Tucker's breathing picks up and I hear him swallow. By the time we reach the old footbridge, he's beyond winded. When he begins to cough into his hand here and there, I glance around quickly, seeing a place to rest. "I often stop here and sit awhile. Would you mind?"

Though his "we can sit" is nonchalant, I can practically feel his relief as he settles down on the edge of the little bridge beside me. Whether or not he knows that I'm lying, he doesn't let on.

The small creek gurgles in front of us and is so clogged with old leaves, that the water is several different shades of glittering gold and orange. Minnows dart about and water bugs skate on top. Tucker watches them with me. Remembering that I didn't eat what's packed in my dinner pail, I pull out a bundled napkin and open it to reveal shelled pecans. I offer Tucker some and we bite into them, throwing little pieces into the water to see if we can hit a minnow or two. Tucker has very good aim.

He talks about how he used to fish here with his friends and even points toward a shady spot up a ways where he vows trout like to hide. When I ask about those friends, he shrugs it off. When I gently press, he finally confides that they decided to keep their distance. He mumbles something about superstition and ignorance, and my heart hurts over that.

"Which is something else that I like about you," he says after biting a pecan in half.

I peer over at him.

He studies it a moment, as if not ready to continue. "You don't seem scared of me. As if I'm going to make you ill somehow. That's...not common." His eyes find mine. "Thank you."

The edges of my throat squeeze in. My chest aches that people would treat him that way. I can see that he's unwell, and while he hasn't told me what it is, I haven't been worried at all that he might make me sick. I couldn't take it if that were the case. The thought of having to separate from him. Perhaps I shouldn't be thinking like this...

A wiser girl might find someone else to be friends with. But I'm not that girl.

He's still looking at me and now the bundle of pecans sits untouched between us. I want to thank him as well. Because he doesn't make me feel like I'm invisible. Walking home with boys isn't something I've done frequently. Only one other time—with Samuel Fischer. It was during our last month in South Carolina. He asked me and I said yes, but in the end, he just wanted an excuse to see Maggie. Samuel just stared at her as she was washing clothes in the yard and I went inside without saying goodbye. At church the next Sunday, he asked her to go driving with him.

I have a feeling Tucker isn't aiming to see Maggie. But I don't really know. I guess I'll find out when we get there.

As if knowing it's time to head on, Tucker slowly rises. Reaching down, he helps me stand and I can see in the tightening of his eyes what it costs him. The gesture warms me right through.

The creek gurgles a little farewell as I tuck my things back into my dinner pail, and Tucker offers me the lead on the footbridge. "It has a pretty sound," I say as we cross.

Tucker agrees that it does. We walk another minute in silence. "If life had a sound, if it was an instrument, what would it be to you?"

I'm getting used to his odd ideas, so I ponder his words seriously. "I'm not sure. Perhaps a harp?"

"Why do you say it like a question? It's your

opinion, not mine."

"I *suppose* it sounds like a harp." I step off the bridge into the soft earth of the forest floor. "And what would you say?"

He steps up beside me. "I say it sounds like the cavalry."

"The cavalry?"

He stops walking, and over his shoulder I see my house in the far distance. Maggie is in the yard, tugging dried clothes from the line. Her skirts are full—more grown-up looking than my own—and her apron strings bounce prettily as she reaches out for another pin. Tucker has turned to watch her as well. My heart sinks.

"Is that your sister?" he asks.

I can only nod, which is just fine because he's glancing back to me.

"I saw her in church the first week you were here. I don't think you saw me. My folks and I were in the back." He shifts his boots. "But I could hear you singing. Both of you. I have to say, I like your voice the best of anyone else."

Despite everything that was just dipping inside me, a rising comes and I can't help but smile. Speckled light is soft on his shoulders, brightening one side of the face that's peering down at me.

"You were mentioning something about the cavalry," I say in a small voice.

"Oh, yeah. I think there are times that life sounds like that. Like twenty brass bugles. Thirty drummers. A building…as if something is about to happen." He gently takes my elbow and turns me a little so the sunlight poking through the treetops hits me full on. His eyes close. "Can you hear it?" he whispers.

Warmth puddles onto my hair, down my shoulders. Everywhere. I stare at him, trying so hard to hear it, all the while wanting to ask God if there's some way we can make this boy well. That I'm having a hard time imagining a world without him.

His eyes are still closed, voice soft and near. Just for me. "I heard the cavalry when you sat beside me that first day."

Still staring up at him, I have no idea why I told him he wasn't good at speaking to girls.

FIVE

The next day in school, I read my graded essay and am pleased by Mr. Davis' comments. I don't know why I thought him so scowly and grumpy when I first met him. He is a rather good man. Especially in the way he pulls the stool up to Tucker's side in the back of the classroom and listens while he conjugates verbs in Greek. I have no idea what Tucker's saying, and half the time I don't think Mr. Davis does either.

They switch to Latin and Tucker plucks up that book. He pulls a marker from the pages and sets it on the desk. Some kind of postcard with a printed drawing of a bird. It's scuffed and has been folded who knows how many times, but the elegant text is still readable. *His eye is on the sparrow*.

It's a comforting thought. I find myself wanting to touch it. Wanting to look over at Tucker and better know the boy who carries it around with him.

Mr. Davis adjusts his stool. "Let's begin with the

second conjugation verbs." He flips forward a few more pages in Tucker's book. "All right....*doceō, -ēre, docuī, doctum.*"

Tucker stares down at the desk. "To teach."

"Correct. Now...*cubō, -āre, cubuī, cubitum.*"

Tucker wets his lips and his eyes close in concentration. "To lie down."

The gentle way he says the phrase makes every word I've ever uttered seem clumsy. He and Mr. Davis continue this exchange for another few minutes and I stare at the open text in front of me, trying very hard to appear busy as I listen to Tucker's voice responding to a language I don't know.

"And the new ones?" Mr. Davis asks. "That you've been working on?" Glasses on the end of his nose, Mr. Davis peers down at the book.

I stare at Tucker.

"Let's see..." Tucker leans back and clasps his hands behind his head. He squints his eyes closed tight again, and just like the other day, I can practically feel how hard he's thinking. He speaks slowly, his voice almost distant. "*Maneō, -ēre, mansī, mansum*...to wait for." He clears his throat. "*Teneō, -ēre...tenuī, tentum.*" His chest rises and falls with each word and he leans back a bit, drawing his shirt taut across his abdomen. "To hold." There's a dash of amusement to the curve of his mouth as he continues with "*ārdeō, -ēre, ārsī'*. To burn." Tucker wets his lips again, eyes still closed. "To be on fire."

Mercy.

I'm mesmerized. And realize it too late when Mr. Davis clears his throat and Tucker opens his eyes to find me hanging on his every word.

"Sarah," Mr. Davis says sternly. "How are you progressing on your own Latin?"

Oh, Latin and I are getting along very well just now.

But I can't say that, so I just say, "Um…" as I peel my gaze away from Tucker's amused expression and face the front of the room. My cheeks are roasting, so I squeak out a request to get a drink of water, and to my blessed relief, Mr. Davis consents. Outside, the afternoon air cools my skin, and at the pump I fill the tin cup and gulp down very unladylike sips.

I manage to return to my seat and bury my nose in the philosophy book that Mr. Davis has lent me. He wants me to read the first three chapters this week, and I decide that with my cheeks still hot, there's no time like the present.

Tucker has finished his Latin recitation by now—

thank God—and likely having already read the book I'm on, is doing some copy work of the Sermon on the Mount. As Mr. Davis explains to the little ones about the French and Indian War, I force myself to focus solely on the pages in front of me.

School goes a few minutes late, so when Mr. Davis finally dismisses everyone, the children rush out. I slam the philosophy book closed. *Really* not wanting to talk to Tucker just now, I hurry out the door. Betsy skips off with the Nettle girls to their neighboring farm since Ma said she could, leaving me to walk home alone.

In my rush, the lace on my petticoat snags on my boot buttons. I have to crouch to free it and am just stepping down the lane again when someone moves in beside me.

"What are your thoughts on geometry?" Tucker asks.

I pause and stare at him.

"How have you done with it so far?"

Still mute, I have to force out words. "What are you doing?"

"Walking you home."

"Why?"

"So…we can talk about geometry." But his smile is impish.

I don't believe him one bit, and I still haven't recovered from earlier, so I don't know what to say. I turn all thoughts to what's at stake for him—the distance it is to my home. "I just don't want you to have to walk me. It's awful far."

"No farther than mine."

"Yes, but you'd have to double back again, so it's twice as far."

"Is that so?" He's humoring me again.

Good gravy. I've never been so unhinged and here he is, making it worse.

"Unless I'm completely offensive to you, I won't take no for an answer." He starts toward my home without me.

"Tucker." I have to jog to catch up. "How about a bargain?"

He looks over at me.

"Why…why don't I walk with you to your house today? So we can talk about geometry," I add, feeling a little embarrassed by all of this. What does it mean, anyway, that he's standing here, trying to make more time with me?

"No. That's all backwards." He shakes his head.

"I thought you wanted me to be more *contingent* in

my thinking," I say, teasing him on his choice of words. "*You* walking *me* home is completely ordinary."

He rolls his eyes, but I can see I'm about to win.

"Plus, you can hear all the cookie recipes I know how to make so you can decide what you'd like." Maybe I haven't landed him hook, line, and sinker on this, but he finally concedes the point and starts in the opposite direction from my home.

"I've been wondering where you live," I add, hoping he doesn't feel bad for me to be the one accompanying him.

"Have you now?" Curiosity laces his voice.

His arm brushes mine as we walk.

We talk about geometry, which doesn't last long—it's not a very exciting subject. But there's something very endearing about him when we do. He talks with his hands and speaks a little too fast and makes all kinds of comparisons that I don't grasp, but I don't really care because I have a reason to watch him.

Cookies come next and I discover that shortbread is his favorite. Shortbread it is.

The lane curves around to the left, leading us across a meadow. Spring grasses lean tall and lanky against us and my hands comb through them as we walk. A wagon rattles down a distant road and a moistness in the air hints at rain. I feel a little hot and clammy, but Tucker seems comfortable in his sweater. Eventually, he does tug off those fingerless gloves of his. He's a slow walker. This is what I notice the most. There's no hurry going anywhere and I have a feeling it's the pain he's in. Though I've never once heard him complain. Maybe I'm just imagining all of it.

Maybe everything's perfectly fine and Tucker truly will be going to college.

But then I remember the way he held his side that first day. The way he needed to rest yesterday. How his breathing is picking up faster than my own just now. We stop for a small break, and while Tucker leans against a tree, I sit beside him, sketching the horizon on my slate. He watches quietly, complimenting it much more than it deserves.

When he seems ready to go on, I tuck my things away and we start back down the path. When we reach the creek, he touches my lower back, letting me go over a little log bridge first. A few minutes later, he turns right on the path, bumping me accidentally when I'm not paying attention.

He clears his throat and I clasp my hands in front of

my skirt.

"Just a bit farther," he says softly.

"This is a pretty area." With the meadow behind us, tiny white flowers in bloom, I can see what a nice place it is to live. Our cabin is surrounded by trees, and while I do like that, this openness is what I grew up with.

He points in the distance to a two-story cabin.

It's made of logs that seem newer than our own. It's large and looks solid. A trickle of smoke rises from the chimney and I'm sure his ma is cooking supper.

"Thank you for walking me," he says rather sheepishly. "Are you sure you're gonna be all right going home alone? I'm a bit worried about you."

"Absolutely. It's plenty light and I enjoy walking."

He doesn't seem convinced, but it's true.

Yesterday, I bid him goodbye at our well where I fetched him a drink of water. Today he suggests the same, so I follow him that way. He hoists up a bucket and fills a tin cup that dangles on a sun-bleached string. I sip, then give it to him and he finishes it off. He wipes his mouth with the back of his hand, watching me.

I smile, wishing I didn't have to bid him farewell.

"Who's this, Tucker?"

We both turn to see a silver-haired woman standing

on the porch, drying her hands on her apron. He introduces her as his ma. She's farther along in years than my own mother, but I suppose that if Tucker is the baby of the family, it makes sense.

"Pleasure to meet you, Mrs. O'Shay," I say.

"And this is Sarah." He motions toward me. "The girl I'm tutoring."

His ma comes down the steps and extends a hand. "I've heard so much about you." She has a pretty drawl.

Tucker grimaces. I smile.

"Have you thought of inviting her for supper tomorrow, Tucker?"

He shakes his head slowly, his face coloring.

Mrs. O'Shay looks to me. "We're havin' a small party for Tucker. It's his birthday."

I glance at him and he's ducked his head to kick at a pebble.

"Won't you come?" she asks. "It'd be so nice to have one of his school chums there." She looks at him in that knowing way that only mothers have.

"Thanks, Ma," he grumbles.

"I'd love to," I say.

Tucker glances at me and I hope he sees how much I mean it.

S I X

My parents' bedroom is at the back of our cabin. It's a small, cozy room and has the only mirror in the house. Standing here this evening, peering at my reflection, I hope I look all right.

Tucker wasn't in school again today, which was much easier to bear knowing that it's likely nothing serious. He *has* done this before. And I get to spend the evening with him. A thrill rushes through me every time I think about it. I have a tin of fresh shortbread sitting on the kitchen table, tied with a scrap of white fabric as a bow. It's all I can do on such short notice, but I think he'll be pleased.

He's going to be eighteen. Though I'm sixteen, I've only been so for a few months. I've never worn my hair up, but there's something about all of this that has me pinning it up off my neck in the fashionable pile I've seen Maggie do many times. In fact, she's watching me in the mirror. She steps in to help when I struggle, and the finished effect is rather pretty. She asks me a few questions about Tucker, but I don't answer her as well as she'd like. I ask about the man from the post office—a Mr. Sawyer, I've since learned. She answers about as evasively. Talking about the opposite sex is never something we've been good at with one another.

Ma breezes in and helps straighten my collar before giving me a kiss on the cheek. She tells me how pretty I look as she glimpses my reflection in the mirror. Her eyes—the same color as mine—smile kindly. The little lines I love, crinkling in that way of hers. I note again how much younger she is than Tucker's own mother. She married my pa when she was fourteen. Three weeks after her father sold him a horse. He's five years older than her, and they're so in love that I couldn't imagine a time that they didn't know one another. Though I realize that this isn't how it works for all people, their story is never far from my mind and I doubt it's far from Maggie's either. Ma squeezes me again then slips downstairs. Maggie steps near so she can fiddle a bit more with my hair.

When she's done, I stare at the result in the mirror. It's strange to see myself looking grown up. Turning my head from side to side, I give my cheeks a quick pinch, try to ignore my blaring lack of curves, and sigh. I should be going. Tin in hand, I thank Maggie and hurry down the stairs where I bid farewell to Ma and Betsy. My mother has made me promise that I'll have someone drive me home since Pa is in Mount Airy with the wagon. I assure her again that I will.

The walk to Tucker's takes longer than I anticipate and I fear I'm late by the time I reach his drive.

Someone's sitting on his porch steps and I realize it's him when he stands.

His hands are fisted at his sides and his blue eyes are wide as I draw near. "I'm sorry you got suckered into this."

"Say something like that again and I'm not going to give you your cookies."

The words register briefly in his expression, but honestly, he's just staring at me now.

Discreetly, I touch my hair, then check to make sure my white blouse is tucked into Maggie's best skirt. Did I overdo it?

His throat dips and he wets his lips that have more color today. Or maybe his skin is just a little paler. "You look very pretty," he says softly. His sandy blond hair is combed off to the side, but that stubborn bit in the front pokes up a tad. He's wearing a crisp, white shirt.

"Thank you. You look nice yourself." Not sure what to do now, I hand him the tin of cookies. "Happy birthday."

His smile is so sweet that it binds my heart tight.

Then he ushers me up the stairs and holds the front door open. I slip inside and his house smells good. Like roast chicken and something yeasty fresh from the oven. The lower level is one big room, encompassing a living area, dining table, and kitchen. A fire is crackling in the woodstove. His family all seems to be there, and I recognize their faces from church. Tucker makes quick work of the introductions and I'm soon putting names to those faces.

His brother Benjamin is only a few years older than Tucker but has a beard that brushes his chest. Benjamin's young wife looks about Maggie's age and shakes my hand amiably. Her name is Violet and a round bump in her tummy only adds to the sweet blush in her cheeks. They live here and I imagine they'll one day have this house. They look happy. Mary is the oldest of the three and seems shy, but she smiles kindly. Tucker has told me that she's thirty and I quickly learn that she's betrothed to a farmer in Franklin County.

There are others. A woman I meet is his Aunt Sue—a

widow. Tucker's pa is as kind as his ma, and the gray-haired man has blue eyes that sparkle just like his youngest son's.

I shake everyone's hand and his mother declares that supper is about ready. At the cloth-covered table, Tucker pulls a chair out for me and I sit, feeling very much like a lady. He sits beside me and I love how normal that feels.

Mr. O'Shay prays for the meal, thanking the Lord for Tucker and the blessing he is to their family. Everyone is holding hands, which means that Tucker's skin is warming around mine. After the amen, Mrs. O'Shay passes me a dish of green beans. I take a small helping then offer it to Tucker who scoops a bunch onto his plate before passing the dish to his brother.

"I'm glad to see you eating, Tuck," his sister says.

He hasn't been eating? I glance over at Tucker. In the candlelight, the shadows beneath his eyes look more pronounced.

He gives his sister a sharp look that answers my question. "I just wasn't hungry the last day or so. But tonight…" He takes the bread basket and offers me a warm roll before taking two for himself. "Ma made all my favorites." He glances at me and winks.

We eat and the food is delicious. I vow to never tell

Ma that Mrs. O'Shay is a better cook, but it's no wonder that these are all Tucker's favorites. Conversation never wanes and Tucker is always in the center of it all. He's clever and makes everyone laugh in a way that has you glad to know him.

When plates are emptied, Aunt Sue and Benjamin's wife clear them away. I offer to help and they chat easily with me as we carry things to the washbasin. Within minutes, the tablecloth is emptied. Gifts appear when Mary slips them from a cupboard beneath the stairs. She arranges them ceremoniously in front of Tucker as everyone makes a show of *ooh*-ing and *ahh*-ing while he grins bashfully.

He starts with the middle-sized package. A few new books. He reads the titles and seems pleased, then thanks his aunt heartily. Next, he tears into the smallest one. It's a box that takes him a few moments to shimmy open, and when he does, his fingers still. Expression going slack.

There's a light clinking sound and then he's pulling out what look like thin glass plates. Embedded in the glass are paper labels. They don't make any sense to me, but Tucker is staring at them with his mouth hanging open.

His mother beams and peers over at her husband who is watching Tucker with glistening eyes.

Finally, Tucker speaks. "You *didn't*." Quickly and gingerly, he sets the box of glass plates aside and moves to the larger package that's about as tall as the width of his shoulders. He tears into the paper, revealing a polished wooden box. He mutters to himself, and turning the box onto its side, unlatches it. I don't know what's in there. I can't look away from his face—the awe. The utter, boyish wonder.

A smile bubbles up inside me.

Then he's lifting something out that's brassy, shiny, and has knobs. I realize instantly what it is—a microscope. I've only seen them in catalogs or heard about them in textbooks. The light hits it beautifully and I wonder if they are expensive.

Tucker's eyes are wide and he shifts his gaze to his brother. "Shooter."

Benjamin speaks cool and slow. "What about him?"

"Is this why you sold your horse, Benjamin?"

"No. He wasn't that good of a horse."

Slowly, Tucker shakes his head and pushes the microscope away a little. "I can't accept this."

Benjamin smirks. "I *can't* get that horse back, even if I wanted to, which I don't. And that microscope ain't goin' nowhere. Besides, no one would want it now with your fingerprints all over it."

Tucker's pa laughs loudly, and despite myself, I giggle. Tucker grins at me then at his brother.

"This is too much," Tucker mumbles, still smiling, and I can see he's resigned. He reaches for the smaller box again that must be slides. He pulls one out and holds it up to the light, then shows me so I can do the same. I don't know what I'm looking at, but my gaze moves away from the glass slide to the young man beside me, who's watching it too.

Everything is perfect.

The last word—*perfect*—accidentally slips out, and Tucker looks at me, leaning nearer. Never have his eyes been so close to mine.

"That's one of the perks of having a birthday," he says back, but I can see so much more living in his expression.

"You know what's another perk of havin' a birthday?" his pa says.

Tucker grimaces. "Let's not…"

"Oh, but we must," his sister chirps in. She's not as shy as I thought.

Tucker drops his head in his hands and mumbles good-naturedly. "See what you started?"

"*I* started?" I have no idea what's going on.

"I'll begin." His pa leans against the armrest of his chair with a grin I can see even through the gray beard he's tugging on. "Last September. Tuck by the woodpile."

"All right...that..." Tucker says, pointing at his father, "was not my fault." But he's chuckling and I wonder what the story could possibly be. I don't have to wonder long. His pa dives into the tale and I can almost see Tucker running with all his might from a pile of rolling logs. Before his pa is finished, I'm laughing so hard that I have to wipe my eyes with a napkin. Tucker is red as a beet and just shakes his head slowly.

I elbow him. "I didn't know you were so clumsy."

"I have my moments."

Benjamin's wife, Violet, goes next. "Christmas," she says with a twinkle in her eye. "In the mudroom. With the raccoon."

"Now that," Tucker leans forward, pointing at her, "is not a story you're about to tell."

Everyone joins in, talking at once, and it's so lively I can *feel* the joy.

Tucker's laughing, but he's clearly mortified. "I was completely traumatized afterwards."

His brother reminds him that he screams like a girl.

Tucker leans toward me, his mouth so near to my ear that I'm certain I can feel it. "This is why I don't bring friends here," he whispers.

Everyone settles and then his pa looks at his wife. "Mama?"

The room grows slowly quiet. She glances at Tucker and already her eyes are damp. A few seconds pass and she doesn't even blink. "Every moment is my favorite."

All three of her children burst out with how she says that every year and she covers her mouth with the edge of her apron to hide her sheepish smile.

"And it's always true. They're all my favorite." She looks at Tucker—her baby—and her eyes shine.

I swallow a lump in my throat.

Tucker tugs at the front of his hair and glances down at the table a moment. As if needing a few seconds of her own, his mother rises and is gone just a few minutes. She returns with a cake that has a small candle in the middle. She declares that it's chocolate. We sing a song that makes Tucker smile like a child and he blows out the candle. His sister cuts slices and passes them out, and I'm now taking the first bite of chocolate cake I've ever had.

But it's the young man beside me that makes this night unforgettable. The people who love him.

Tucker leans in to whisper again. "Do you hear the cavalry?"

I smile and whisper back that I do.

Benjamin tells me he'll take me home. Though I feel bad that he has to go out of his way to do this, everyone assures me that it's no trouble. It's dark, so I am glad not to walk. And I did promise my mother. I can tell Tucker wants to come, but I can see how tired he is. He hasn't gotten out of his chair in the last little while. Not even to test his microscope that got moved to the far end of the table. He's just now easing to a stand, so I tell him to rest up and that I'll see him at church on Sunday. Though he's clearly disappointed to stay behind, there's a hint of relief there as well.

"I'll see you soon," he promises as he follows me onto the porch.

I walk down the steps behind Benjamin. "See you soon."

He already told me that he would certainly be going to school on Monday and I rest in that as I climb onto the wagon seat. He waves as his brother slaps the reins and an old gray pulls the wagon down the drive. Turning in my seat a little, I wave.

On the drive, Benjamin makes polite talk, and in the few hours I've known him, I like him. He and Tucker make good brothers.

The night is quiet and cool. I settle back against the seat for the mile or so ride home. My hair feels flat—any type of fashionable bun only a memory—and I wonder if that's why women wait until they're older to worry about such things.

I'm too young to wear my hair up and maybe even too young to be thinking about happily ever afters. But I'm doing it anyway. Every vision includes Tucker now.

And that's what scares me.

I fold one arm across my stomach and try to chase away the night's chill. I think back to the card he had in his Latin book. *His eye is on the sparrow.* I've heard that saying before, but never paid too much attention to it. Now, as the wagon prattles on beneath the star-studded sky…I'm holding on to it mighty tightly.

S E V E N

He promised he would be in school and he's not. He also didn't go to church.

I stare out the window. It's sprinkling softly but nothing that might have hindered him should he have been able to come. My feet fidget as the hours wear on, and when two o'clock finally trickles in, I can scarcely grab up my things quick enough to dart out the door, when Betsy reminds me that Ma told us to be home right after school. Groaning, I turn away from the path that leads toward Tucker's and follow my sister home.

The next morning, I make sure and get permission to be home a little late after school. The day drags on so slow, each hour feels worse than the one before. When everyone is dismissed, I snatch up my things and start off again. I wave to Betsy who sings out a farewell as she walks arm in arm with the neighbor girls.

I run down the lane, knowing the way to his house by heart. I wonder how long it's stood there. How long he's lived there. How many birthdays he blushed through around that kitchen table and how many more he might have. I'm breathing hard as I rush on.

Fortunately, the rain has stopped, so I'm quite dry, but my hair is a disaster when I reach his drive. My braid that was bound so neatly this morning is a frayed mess. Slowing to catch my breath, I realize that I ran the whole way here.

I'm exhausted but won't be able to breathe properly until I see that he's fine.

Then I spot him. Sitting on the front porch steps, his microscope beside him. He holds a slide up to the light and doesn't seem to notice me drawing near.

I gulp a few breaths of air, needing it desperately just now. "Why did you do that?"

He lowers the slide and looks at me. His expression is surprised, but he masks it quickly. "Do what?"

"Not come. To school." I can barely breathe. "For two days."

Still studying me, he makes no move to stand and I don't sit. He sighs, letting it out slowly. Not quite looking at me.

Something's changed in him. I can feel it and it scares me.

"Why does it matter?" he finally says.

Still panting, I have to process those words a few times before they make a shred of sense. *"Because I care."*

He nods a little, seeming disappointed. If this were a test, I just answered wrong.

"You promised you would come."

"And I couldn't get there." His gaze holds mine, tightly.

My voice is so small. "You what?"

"I couldn't get there." He looks away again. "I don't *walk* to school, Sarah. Benjamin takes me. He's been taking me for weeks."

Misunderstanding must show in my face.

"Picking me up too."

Someone might as well have punched me, so quickly my chest deflates. He's been walking with me…when he shouldn't have? I swallow hard, trying to put this together. The sight of him on the footbridge, his smile for me as we slowly stroll through the woods. "Tucker." Why didn't he tell me? Not wanting to cry right now, I try to think of how to encourage him. "M—maybe we can ride home together. If you don't mind, I'll come with you—"

"No." His brows dig in. "Don't you see—" There's a

clatter in the kitchen, and when the sounds settle, Tucker grips his wrist with his other hand, resting that forearm on his raised knee. "Benjamin can't take me anymore." Blue eyes stare at my feet as he speaks. "He has to leave before dawn now with the wagon."

"Maybe I could have my pa—"

"Stop it, Sarah." Not looking at me, Tucker pushes his microscope away a little, then places his slides into their box.

With his silence, I don't know what to do or say to try and make it better—or to make it go away—so I just motion toward the stairs beside him. "May I sit with you?" I hate that it sounds like a plea.

"I don't need anyone to sit with me."

That hurt. I realize it must show.

He motions to me. "This is the problem—". There's another clatter from the house and Tucker looks flustered—as if he wants to have this conversation somewhere else. The fact that we can't, the way he's still sitting, is needling through my last shreds of hope.

"You never should have come to my house and met my family," he finally says. "You certainly shouldn't have come to my birthday. Or have been my friend."

I clench my jaw tight to keep my chin from

trembling.

"I'm not going to school anymore. It's all done with."

There's a ripping in my heart as those days skitter into memories.

A tear slides from the side of my eye.

He looks frustrated. "Do you know how wrong all this is?" he asks. "What you really need to do is go on home…and just forget about all of this." He arcs a hand—as if that easy motion can erase *everything*.

The stinging comes stronger. It trickles into my lungs, making me have to fight to get my chest to rise and fall. I don't know what to say to that, so I speak around it. "I was worried about you."

"Please don't worry about me. That's my mother's job."

I flinch and he seems to know how he's hurting me.

"Honestly, I'm fine."

"*Fine*? How fine?"

His brows dip, face lowered, and he peers at me this way. "I don't want to talk about it."

He's fighting. I'm going to let him because I know he needs to free this.

"I want to be your friend, Tucker." Always.

He looks away. "Go home, Sarah."

Another tear slips and I brush it away. Slowly, I nod. There's nothing else I can think of except the truth. "I'll miss you."

His gaze still on the distance, a muscle trips in his jaw. Finally, looking down, he rubs his forehead with his palm. It's easier to step away when I can't see his face, so I turn.

My dinner pail bumps my leg as I walk. I forgot I was holding it. His dirt drive seems much too long, and having run here, all that energy that kept me going the last two days, that got me here so quick, has vanished. My legs are shaking. I want to lie down and cry, but I have to keep walking because I can't stay here.

Despite my best efforts, tears well and the whole world blurs. I press my palms to my eyes, but it does little good. Air is hard to draw in and I try to tell myself that maybe tomorrow will be different. Or maybe the next day. But perhaps those days won't even have him in them. A sob slips out and I whisper his name. Rounding the bend, the coolness of the shady creek draws me deeper...and I hear him calling my own.

I drop my pail and swipe my eyes with a sleeve. I glance back and he calls it again. I can't see him. Then there's a rustle beyond the stand of trees behind me and it's him.

He walks quickly, his gait uneven, jaw clenched with such clear pain, fresh tears rush me. I start toward him and nearly stumble when he struggles to jog. I want to tell him to stop, that I'm coming, but a rising sob makes it impossible. The next thing I know, I'm running so quick, I could very well collide with him if I don't stop. My shoes skid to a halt in front of his in a way that makes me feel like a little girl. But he's not looking at me like I'm a little girl.

He's doubling over a bit, his hurting so clear that it pierces straight through me.

"Why did you do that?" I sob.

"I'm sorry," he pants. "I'm *so* sorry."

I'm trying to support his weight, and he's trying to straighten, and we become a tangled mess that makes no sense until he kisses me. His skin is hot from his running and his lips are the softest thing I've ever known. A little cry slips from my throat.

His hand slides to the back of my head. It's not a kiss that's shy and fast like I would have done. It's sweet and so tender that the legs that were failing me moments ago are about to buckle. As if knowing as much, his other arm wraps around my middle, holding me tightly. His fingertips press into the flesh above my hipbone. A corner of my heart cries out that he shouldn't be holding me this way. Supporting me. His pain flashes through my mind and I quell the thought, forcing myself to trust him as I bring my arms over his shoulders, around his neck. I've always thought he seemed strong, but this is the first time my hands know how much.

And suddenly everything is right with the world and everything is wrong with it.

I haven't realized just how tall he is until now that he's bending to kiss me. Or is he this way because he's hurting? I try not to think of the reason—what the doctors may have told him—and simply savor the warmth of his mouth on mine. His hands hold me tighter. I've never kissed a boy. Not ever, and *certainly* not like this.

Things may be getting a bit carried away. Especially in the middle of the path in the middle of the day, but I don't care. He seems to have forgotten that the rest of the world exists. That's when I feel him wince. It's more of a cringe, but he tries to fight it and kisses me again. It lasts mere seconds when he cringes once more.

"Ow," he breathes.

The single sound is so flooded with agony that I pull

away. "Tucker."

He groans and, with one hand gripping my forearm, doubles over, his other palm pressed to his thigh. He groans again.

He's sinking to his knees and I follow.

"Please don't." He pushes me upright, then his hands meet the dirt. He sits back on his heels and is grimacing so hard a burn pricks my eyes. He lowers himself to his forearms so that his face is just inches from the ground. He's struggling to even breathe and I don't know if I should try and help him or run and fetch someone.

"Should I get someone?" It nearly comes out as a whimper.

"No!" he pants. "I just need…a second. Please."

I sink to the ground anyway. "What's wrong?" Now I am crying. I will beg him to tell me if I have to.

Despite everything, he begins to chuckle and I'm utterly confused. "Calm down, Sarah. I'm fine." Then he mumbles that this is beyond embarrassing. "I shouldn't have ran like that…and…you…"

With my legs folded under me, I sit back and wait. The seconds drag on like an eternity, but it's surely less than a minute when he finally sits up more.

He's still bent over, but he manages to look sideways

at me. "You're gonna kill me." Using his sleeve, he wipes at sweat on his brow. This is the first time I've seen him this way—flushed, skin glistening.

In confirmation, he begins to tug up the front of his sweater with one hand, still using his other against the dirt for balance. I rise to help him, pulling his sweater up his hot back and easing it past his shirt, then over his head where the slight curl of his hair is damp at the nape of his neck. We somehow manage to get his arms free and he's panting again when I finally bundle the wool in my hands.

"Thank you." He glances over at me and sits back, looking somewhat recovered.

"Please tell me what's hurting you." That seems a silly way to phrase it, but I'm telling myself here and now that he's not dying. I have to.

"Would it be too much to keep some details to myself?" He swipes at his forehead again. "I've already had doctors poking and prodding where they don't belong and now…" His Adam's apple dips and he looks at the ground. "It's just not somethin' that I want to talk about with people, let alone a girl…especially *you*."

Part of me wants to make sense of what he's saying, but I focus on his face. "The pain…"

He gasps for breath a moment then squints over at

me. "It's mostly here." He touches his lower abdomen. "And here." His broad hand slides to his lower back, then he says something about his legs that's so brief, I don't quite catch it.

"I'm so sorry."

He struggles to his feet and I grip his arm, trying to help. To my relief, he's not holding onto me much and I pray he's not trying to be brave.

"Let's get you inside."

He nods. His hand finds mine, his fingers entwining with my own, and he's holding it so tenderly, my heart breaks.

"I promise not to kiss you like that again," I say.

"Now that," he gulps but seems to be recovering some, "is a world I don't want to live in."

I smile into his shoulder—*hating* his humor—feeling the heat in his skin. The way his shirt clings. "Then maybe just little kisses."

"I suppose I could live with that...most of the time."

Our pace is slowing and he seems a bit unsteady now. I slide my arm around his waist and try to support him. His sweater is still in my grip and his skin is cooling. But his shirt is still damp. He's trembling now.

I draw the sweater closer to him. "Should you put

this back on?"

"Let's just get into the house," he pants.

So we do. We make it to a wide bench in the living area and he sits on it, looking a little sheepish as he leans sideways on his hip, pulling his legs up, lying down like a child who's home sick from school. I snag a pillow from the rocker to shimmy under his head. His mother rushes in and I step back as she drapes a blanket over him, asking what's happened.

"Just overdid it," he responds.

"What can I get you?" she asks.

He answers her, but I don't hear. I just step farther back, knowing I don't really belong. His brother comes down the stairs then and smiles at me as if not realizing what's happening. Then he spots Tucker on the bench and comes around, kneeling by his little brother. They share quiet words. Again, I don't hear it; I'm trying not to listen. Their faces are close together, voices deep and direct, and I know it's not a conversation for me.

Benjamin rises, promising to fetch something for Tucker. I know this is my cue to go home. But I can't bring myself to move. Can't pull my eyes from his face, so afraid am I that this is the end. There's a big part of me that doesn't think it is, but I can't risk turning away and finding out.

I lower myself beside him and hate the expression he has. There's embarrassment there, as if he's done something wrong.

"May I visit you tomorrow?" I touch the edge of his blanket. "After school?"

"You don't have to." Tucker shifts to lie on his back.

"I *want* to." And I desperately want him to know that he's not going to scare me away. I'm not about to give up on him. With only the two of us in the room, I press the softest kiss I can manage to his lips and feel him smile. "Tomorrow. Please."

His eyes are wide and vulnerable when he looks at me, and I see a rush of gratitude. Almost hope. He nods. "I'll see you soon. Do good in school."

"See you soon," I say softly.

His ma bustles in carrying a cup of water and an extra blanket. Her eyes are slightly red and I realize it didn't take very long to fetch that water. A mother's heart has no doubt been spilling silently out by the water pump. My own chin trembling, I bid Tucker goodbye and force myself to leave.

EIGHT

Having begun an accidental staring contest with the far wall, I almost fall out of my chair Wednesday morning when Ma says Tucker's name over breakfast, bringing me back to earth.

I'm pretty sure I blush three shades of red. "What?"

Without answering, she gives me a knowing look and goes back to clearing dishes. But she's smiling. Last night, as I sat on her bed and she ran the bristle brush through my hair, I told her what happened at Tucker's. That he'd kissed me...

And while I didn't say much about it, I didn't have to because Ma's eyes were shining as she plaited my hair. Betsy, who was lounging beside me, giggled, and I knew it was best to change the subject. I asked Betsy if she liked the new hymn we learned at church. When we couldn't quite recall all the words, Ma sang it for us.

Realizing that I'm staring at the wall again, I dash upstairs to find my shoes while Betsy fusses in the doorway about being late to school. She soon mellows as we start off with enough time to get there. I straighten my skirt and the wind plays in the maples while Betsy chats easily.

At school, the little building is abuzz with students discussing the fall break, even though it's still a few months away. As eager as I am to not have to sit in this place without Tucker, I'm also trying desperately not to think of autumn. I don't know what it will hold.

The classroom finally settles, and while most pupils take a silent spelling test, Mr. Davis comes by my desk to bring me a new list of words. He tells me that he visited with Tucker that morning to go over the details of his exam for Brown the following week. This pleases me to no end. Knowing I won't make it through the day otherwise, I pour all my focus onto my studies. It helps with the empty feeling of the seat. The way he's not beside me. I miss everything about him.

Two o'clock can't come fast enough, and when it does, I barrel down the lane, running to his house. I force myself to slow after a minute so I don't break the cookies I baked for him. Through the meadow, then over the little footbridge I walk...and finally spot his house in the distance. Mary waves at me from the garden. Beside her,

Tucker's aunt and Violet pile plucked weeds into a wooden pushcart.

Tucker is there, sitting on the porch where he was yesterday, turning one of the knobs on his new microscope. It's on the step between his boots, propped up on a stack of books. He seems to be trying to figure it out. He peeks into the eyepiece for a long while, his head popping up only when I draw near.

He grins a bit and it's crooked. "You sure got here fast."

A little embarrassed, I nibble my lip a moment. "How are you feeling?"

"Just fine." His shirt hangs untucked around his brown pants and his collar is skewed.

I settle down beside him. "Did you sleep well?"

He turns another knob on his microscope, then moves a glass slide into place. He peers into the eyepiece for several seconds, completely ignoring my question. "Are you gonna come with me on Thursday to the entrance exam?" He looks up. "I know it's kind of far, but Benjamin will drive us over and maybe I can have my ma come if that makes things easier for you. I already talked to Mr. Davis and he said it wouldn't be a problem for you to take the exam as well."

Tucker says this with such hope that I don't want to let him down, but I have to. "I'm afraid I can't."

"If it's money, I'll pay your way. It only costs—"

"Please. I don't want you to."

"I need something to spend it on and I'd rather it be you."

"Please save it." The moment the words slip out, his expression shifts. I know just what he's thinking, so I try to redirect things. "How did you come up with all this money that you aim to spend?"

He smiles a little and I hope it's done the trick. "It's from my working days, the last few years."

"What did you do?"

"You're changing the subject. Will you come with me?"

I sigh. I've never been cut out for this sort of thing. The way he dreams big. As if I can just reach out and grab hold of my hopes. As if I can just make them come true. If that were the case, it would be Tucker I'd be wishing for, not college. "You're asking me to do something that I just can't do."

He sets his mouth and slowly nods. For a moment, I think he's resigned to let this go, but then he peers over at me. "Sarah, sometimes life chooses for us. Other times we'll have to choose for ourselves. It's important to be prepared for both."

"What do you mean?"

"I'm just telling you not to sell yourself short. Whatever it is that you want to do in this life—do it wholeheartedly. Will you promise me that?"

"I'll come with you, but please don't make me take the test."

He looks over at me and I can see he's not unhappy. "I'd never make you do anything you don't want to do." He brushes a bit of hair away from my shoulder, pushing it around the other side, baring my neck. His fingers trail lightly over my dress between my shoulder blades, before his hand falls away.

"But I will come with you," I whisper, having no idea how I managed words just now. "I'll talk to my folks."

The memory of his touch still lingering, I watch him shift his legs. He winces a bit as he tries to readjust himself. "It's a deal. Say...how about we move to the rockers."

I rise and it takes all my strength to not try and help him as he struggles to his feet. I walk ahead of him to the rocking chairs on the far end of the porch, that way he won't feel as if I'm watching him. He nudges them together so the wooden armrests touch.

When we're both settled, he speaks as if there was no lull. "Tell me something." Leaning against the headrest, his eyes close briefly. I can see that he's tired. "What are your favorite activities? I have a whole list of questions for you, so we may as well start there."

I bring my legs up so I can curl myself closer to him. His hair flips up in the front, and wanting to be helpful, I try to smooth it down as I ponder, but just end up poking it up more because I like it that way. "I enjoy reading. And drawing. And being outdoors. I used to like to run. Is that strange? You get places so much faster when you run. I try not to now. It's not very ladylike. But I still do sometimes."

"I like that. You should run whenever you get the urge." His hand squeezes mine.

"What are *your* favorite activities?"

"Um..." He shifts his legs out more so the sun hits them. "Reading. And kissing you."

I smile.

"And being smarter than you."

Now I laugh.

"These aren't in order, of course, or I would have

started with the kissing part." He flashes me a look that does tipsy things to my insides. "I also like trying to make sense of Reverend Gardner's sermons. They're actually quite good once you figure out what he's talkin' about. Oh, and I like to be late to school."

"That's a terrible hobby."

"Ain't it?" He chuckles.

But when he hisses in a breath and shifts his legs again, I hope with all my heart that he can be late to his college classes. I hope the professor chides him something fierce, and that Tucker settles down at a desk in the back to hide his mischievous smile.

I hope this with all my heart.

But he winces again as he tries to get comfortable. Perhaps he would be in bed if it weren't for me.

"Should we go inside?" I ask softly. "Would you be more comfortable if you laid down?"

Something flickers through his expression as his chest rises and falls. "If I do that…I'll never be back." He slow-shakes his head and looks at me when I take his hand in mine. "My world is already small. I fear it will be nothing if I do that."

I trace my thumb across his palm. When he's quiet, I think of something to distract him with. "This is a pretty view here."

Reaching over with his other hand, he brushes a bit of my hair behind my ear. "It is."

I glance over to see him looking at me. I suddenly feel shy, but I really ought not to be. "What did you do before your favorite hobby was being smarter than me?"

"I"—he shifts again—"I worked at the sawmill after school."

"Did you?" I can picture this. There's a wholeness to it.

"I enjoyed it. It was hard work, but I liked that about it." He shifts again, adjusting his boots.

"Are your legs bothering you?"

I can practically feel a lie surface when he squints at me, but then he blinks and those same eyes grow rounder. More vulnerable. "A bit."

"Is there anything I can do for you? Or get you?"

"Nope." He takes up my hand again. "Just being here…" He peers over toward the skyline where the sun is tinting the tops of the trees a pale gold and we sit there a long while without speaking.

His thumb traces slow circles over my own.

Fearing I may doze off, I make myself sit up a little. "I'm going to do my next essay on Thomas Jefferson."

He looks over at me.

"I confess, I've never paid much attention to who ran our country, but I find it more interesting now. Especially since I'm friends with a future president. I don't want to be a complete dunce when I can finally say that 'I knew you when.'"

His smile is so immediate…so sincere…it fills my heart and breaks it all at the same time.

"That's a good idea," he says, a light still in his eyes. "If you need help, I know everything there is to know about Mr. Jefferson."

"Do you?"

"Yep."

I hunt for a fact I recently read to impress him with. "So, are you aware that he had eleven grandchildren?"

"Actually, he had twelve. He also liked vanilla ice cream and writing letters."

Drat.

Tucker bobs his brows. "You're welcome to put that in your essay, if you want to."

Without thinking, I reach over and shove his shoulder playfully. The moment I do, I feel terrible. But then he reaches over and shoves me back. It makes everything better.

Still chuckling, he settles against his rocker and closes his eyes a moment. "I hope you do some reading on the First Ladies while you're at it. There were some truly remarkable women."

"I'll do that."

"Good." He takes my hand and pulls it across his chest, draping it on his far shoulder so that I'm leaning against his side. "And just so you know, you would make an excellent First Lady." He gives me one of those dashing looks of his. The kind that turns me to mush. Lifting my fingers, he kisses them.

NINE

Two days later, I sit in my kitchen, peeling potatoes and thinking of how Tucker is on his way to Danville for his exam. I had asked my ma and pa if I could go, but because of the distance—and the impropriety that presented—there was no way. Tucker and his brother would be staying in a hotel at least a few times along the way, and his ma wasn't able to come along.

They're completely right, but still, disappointment rolls around in my mind while I skin a potato, so I try to turn that feeling into something else. I turn it into prayers for Tucker. That he would have safe travels. That he would arrive on time for his test on Monday. And that he would do well on his exam. I wonder if he's nervous. If he's cramming Latin and Greek and mathematics into that head of his. I hope not. I hope he's enjoying the sights and the time spent with his brother. They're scheduled to be gone a week.

Tucker told me that they would be meeting someone

called a *proctor* who would administer the exam. I'm so thankful to Mr. Davis for setting this up.

I realize I'm no longer peeling potatoes when Maggie taps a wooden spoon a little louder than necessary on the edge of the pot she's tending.

I know that if I let it, the week will drag by horrifically slow, so I determine to make myself as useful as possible to make up for all my time away lately. I weed the garden and even wash and iron all the curtains. I quiz Betsy in her studies and go with Pa to Mount Airy where he often does business. Maggie comes along and we visit the post office then fetch some things from the general store. Pa lets me pick out a lavender-scented bar of soap, and Maggie chooses a new handkerchief. We take care to pick out some candy from the jars on the counter for Betsy and both snag a piece for ourselves.

I manage to keep busy in school by studying new word lists and writing up a handful of essays that Mr. Davis says "get better and better." He asks me what I'd like to write about next, and I respond by asking him what he might want to read.

He gives me a muted smile, then calmly tells me that if I keep answering a question with a question, I'm going to get lost. I'm not sure what that means, but by the end of the day, I stop by his desk and tell him that I'd like to write an essay on the sea and the way it changes with the seasons. I can tell by the light in his eyes that he's pleased.

By the time the week has ended, I find myself walking by Tucker's farm, looking for their wagon. It's not there on Friday. And it's not there on Saturday.

Ma has me stay home after church, which is no matter, for Tucker's wagon is still not there on Monday or Tuesday. By the following day, I'm flying down the road toward his house, praying with all my might the whole way.

It's there in the yard, that sturdy wagon—and my heart lurches into my throat as I hurry up to the front door. Still panting, I set my basket down and knock as politely as I can manage.

Tucker's sister, Mary, answers the door. She wears a sweet smile and says that Tucker is resting.

Never has my heart been so overjoyed as to hear those words. He's home, safe.

"I'll tell him you're here," she says. "Would you like to come in and wait?"

I'm a jumble of nerves, so I offer to wait out on the porch. She nods kindly and leaves the door ajar as she heads for the stairs. The time passes by slowly and I lean on the railing, enjoying the early June breeze. At the sound of footsteps, I turn to see Benjamin come out of the house.

He has a plaid blanket on his arm and greets me warmly.

"Tucker's comin'," he promises. "Sent me out with this." Benjamin tips his head for me to walk on with him.

"How is he doing?" I ask. "How is he feeling? How was his exam?"

Benjamin chuckles a little. "I'm sure he'll tell you all about the test." He walks on a ways, out of the groomed yard and into the tall meadow grasses that surround the house. "As for how he's feelin'…he's a bit tired."

I study Benjamin to try and see what he means by *tired*, but he just fans out the blanket, as if for a picnic, and it settles on the grass. "That should do it." He smiles and it hits me—the blanket.

That's how tired Tucker is. His brother starts back for the house.

"Benjamin?"

"Yep?" He pauses, turning.

"What's ailing Tucker?" I run my thumb over my knuckles, back and forth and back and forth. "What's making him unwell?"

For a few long seconds, Benjamin just tugs on his beard, staring down at his boots. I feel something coming—a dodging of my question—but to my surprise, he looks me square in the eyes. "Have you heard of a sickness called cancer?"

I shake my head.

"It's a disease." He steps forward to straighten a corner of the blanket a moment. "Doctors don't know much about it, but that's what they call it. There are different kinds, I think, but from what I understand, it usually starts in one spot and spreads. That's about all I know." He crams his hands in his pockets and looks off across the meadow. "The kind Tucker has was discovered about thirty years ago." He squints over at me. "I only know this because he's learned everything he can about it. You know Tuck." Benjamin's smile is bittersweet. "In his case, it's… well…" He tugs at his beard again. "Based off what the doctors know and what Tucker tells them, it's spread to his legs…and there's nothin' that can be done about it."

I take those words and hold them loosely. As if the breeze could somehow blow them away.

"The pain is in his bones now."

But they don't go away and I can't draw in air.

Benjamin's beard brushes his shirt as he looks down at the ground. He scuffs his boot.

"Will he…" I swallow hard. "Will he surely…?"

"Die?" he finishes for me. Then Benjamin looks over my shoulder at something.

I glance back to see Tucker coming this way, slowly. The use of a cane helps him along, and I force an inhale when my head gets light.

Sweater tucked under his arm, his face is stony. "What are you doing?" His gaze is so sharp on his brother, I take a small step back.

Benjamin slowly shakes his head. "Tucker—"

"It's my fault," I blurt out.

But Tucker doesn't look at me.

"You should have been tellin' her," Benjamin says.

It's then that I realize that the rosy hue rimming Tucker's lower lids is a little more pronounced. That his gait is slower. His free hand is fisted at his side as if each step hurts.

And what breaks my heart even more is the way he's glaring at his brother. The way he keeps trying to hide it all. "Why don't you mind your own business?" Tucker says to him. He's wearing new-looking brown pants over his scuffed boots, and while his shirt is clean, it's wrinkled. He's gotten the buttons wrong.

I take another little step back.

"Because you're my brother, Tuck. And I care about you, and that makes you my business." Benjamin looks hard at Tucker, then finally says something low that I don't hear. With a small nod in my direction, Benjamin starts away.

Tucker doesn't move for a few moments. He drops the cane off to the side in the grass, then reaches up and grips the back of his neck. Finally, he looks over at me. "I missed you," he says, and I can see how he means it.

"I missed *you*." The words, though the truest thing I've ever spoken, come out small.

"I'm sorry to be mad. I'm real sorry. I'm not mad at you." He peers over to where Benjamin is leaving. In the weight of Tucker's gaze, I see his heart for his brother—his regret. He glances down to the basket that I had set on the blanket.

It's been days since I've seen him, and I've imagined this moment countless times. It never went quite like that in daydreams, and I feel—in the silence—that he's thinking the same thing.

Finally, he speaks. "What did you bring?" I can tell

he's trying to say it cheerily.

I stare a moment at the basket. Then at him. He presses the pad of his thumb to his lips and seems to realize that I'm not going to answer his question until he begins answering mine.

I speak softly, wanting to make this as easy on him as possible. "How bad are you hurting? And what have the doctors said about all this?"

I can tell that he's unhappy, but slowly he eases himself down to sit on the blanket. I settle beside him, touching his arm, needing to feel that he's real.

For a moment, he just pushes the front of his hair off to the side, trying to set it to rights. "Well…" his throat shifts in a swallow. "If you must know…" He doesn't say it unkindly, but I can feel the battle taking place inside him. "The pain has moved into my legs these days." He fiddles with a tatter on the picnic blanket, tracing his thumb over a red stripe in the plaid for a while. "It makes it a bit hard to walk…and stand. Also why I'm gonna have to leave that love of running up to you."

A burning rises in my lungs. "Is there something they can give you? Some medicine? Maybe there's a way—"

"Do we really have to talk about this? How about you tell me how your week was instead."

I don't even move.

Finally, he blows out a sigh. His forehead crinkles and he swipes his fingers over it. "They've given me a few things that help with pain a bit. But…" He shrugs and works his arms into the sleeves of his sweater before pulling it overhead. "It's not much. And no…there's nothing they can do."

"How do you know?" It comes out a plea.

"Because the doctors have already told me." He tugs the blue wool down over his shirt.

I open my mouth to voice some kind of protest— some declaration of how they could be wrong—but I don't even know why I'm trying. His face has gone so somber that every word lodges in my throat.

"It already took my uncle, Sarah."

His words slam into my stomach, shoving out the air. His uncle? My mind flashes back to the night of his birthday when I met his aunt. A widow. Every question I can't form into words must live in my expression, for he takes my hand and holds it in both of his.

"It…would…appear that I have just what my uncle had. The doctors don't quite know what to make of that, but I suppose it could run in families like less complicated things. You know, in the same way that eye color does, or height." The grasses hedging us in and away from the world dance. "This kind only affects men—for reasons that I'm *not* gonna mention." His cheeks color a little, but his eyes are sad. "Probably good that I'll never have a son. Then I won't have to worry about possibly passin' it on."

I try to pull my hand away—needing to cover my face—but he grips it tight, making me look at him.

"I'm just going to say this, all right?" Using his fingers, he spreads out my own so that his hand completely covers mine. "By the time my uncle and everyone realized something was wrong, he only had about a year. That was it. And I'm sorry to tell you, but I've had this for a while now, which means that mine is running out. Pretty quick." He doesn't look up as he talks, just stares at his hand on mine. "There's a procedure that can be done, but it's really risky and frankly, wasn't very appealing, and even if I wanted to try it now…it's too late."

Breathe, Sarah. In. Out.

"I don't want to talk about this anymore," he whispers, then leans back a little. "I could give you all kinds of delightful details about what I have and how *enjoyable* it is, but I'm not going to. I'm just gonna kiss this hand." He lifts mine to his mouth. "And see if you want to take a nap with me." He lowers down to his side, propping his head in his palm, squinting up at me mischievously. "You think we'll get in trouble?" He winks.

With my heart puddling all around, it's all I can do to settle beside him and rest my head in my hand as well.

His fingertips trace up my arm. Then back down. When his hand goes back up again, his fingers slide along my shoulder, to the hollow of my throat. Then his hand slides back behind my neck, into my hair.

"Will you sing me a song?" He kisses me so softly that it's all I can do not to sob.

I have to stay calm. I don't want to waste these moments by coming unglued, and as insane as he's behaving, it makes sense. So I quell all that he told me. Lock it tight in a box and shove the box into the furthest corner of my heart. Where the shadows might cover it from sight. I still know it's there, and it's still killing me, but I make myself look into the blue eyes I've come to love and ask him what song he wants. My words aren't as steady as his own.

"How about a Christmas song? Those are always nice."

Staring down at the plaid blanket, I try and remember what a Christmas song is. Because that locked box isn't staying in the shadows as it should. And Tucker is very slowly pressing measured kisses up my wrist, pushing my sleeve back a little as he does.

"Tucker." My voice is laced with warning, but not enough, because he peers up at me with that rogue grin of his again and goes a little higher, until he reaches the hollow of my elbow.

My head gets so light, it's a good thing I'm laying down.

"Sorry," he says, not sounding like he means it one bit. He settles onto his back and folds his hands behind his head. His eyes fall closed. "Did you think of a song?" He whispers it, sounding tired and doing what he can to hide it. He's been trying to be strong. He's always *being* strong.

Still propped up with my arm, I twine my free fingers back inside his. Clearing my throat, I begin. "O Holy Night. The stars are brightly shining. It is the night of our dear Savior's birth." I sing on, glad the words are ingrained within me and I don't have to think too hard. But when I get to the part about falling on your knees, my voice gets wobbly, throat too tight to go on. Tucker doesn't move. The breeze rustles his hair, and by the gentle parting of his mouth, the soft rise and fall of his chest, he's asleep.

I wait a little while. Just watching him. Savoring the way his blue sweater lifts and lowers with his breaths. The shadows of clouds move across us and the grass sways. Certain he's asleep, I lower myself closer to him, and taking up his hand as gently as possible, nudge up the cuff of his sweater to press a soft kiss to his wrist.

Though his eyes are still closed, I realize he's awake when he smiles.

TEN

The next day I skip school because I can't bring myself to face that place just now. Knowing it's for the best, Ma lets me stay home. Not wanting to barge in on Tucker and his family when they aren't expecting me, I lay on Ma and Pa's bed, holding open a novel that I can't concentrate on. She comes by and brings me something to eat, but it sits untouched on the plate until I finally force myself to eat a few cold bites.

Around one, I head to Tucker's. His pa meets me in the drive and says that Tucker didn't get out of bed today. To come back tomorrow. He says it kindly and gives my shoulder a pat when I tell him goodbye. It's all I can do to keep from crying in front of him. I save that for the footbridge, and it's not until I'm completely spent that I start for home.

Still wiping at my eyes, I take shaky breaths—wishing I wasn't alone. I want Tucker. His smile and his laugh. What would he say to me right now? Probably something horrifically unfunny, which only makes me miss him more, so I try to think instead what someone that I'm not attached to would say. Someone like Reverend Gardner. But that only makes me wonder what God might say.

I squeeze my eyes tight and know what He would say—*do you not trust me?*

My response to that comes easy—*do you not know how much I need Tucker?*

It feels traitorous, but that's the truth. I won't do God the injustice of lying to Him.

And suddenly Mr. Davis' words rush me. *"If you keep answering a question with a question, Sarah, you're going to get lost."*

I *feel* lost.

Walking down the lane, I kick at a small stone and then another. Finally, I pick one up and fling it into the trees. It's not helping. Because Mr. Davis is right. I know he's right. Halting, I sink to a crouch, skirt billowing in the dust. I press my hands to my face and let everything go dark. A slow breath in, a slow breath out.

I don't really feel like praying just now. I don't know what to pray or how to pray for this, but if I could look

God square in the eye right now, I would. I would tell Him how angry I am at Him. For wanting to take Tucker. Does God not realize that I want to grow old with Tucker? I want to sit on the front porch and watch the sunset—listening to his humor. Or simply watch him read. Say vows that make me his. I want to know what it's like to tiptoe upstairs to the sound of crickets and know the feel of his skin. I want to know what it's like to wake up beside him. But I never will.

I want to know his expression if he ever learned he was going to be a daddy.

And I want to scream at God. So I do. Rising, I throw another stone. Then another and another.

I remember the promise *His eye is on the sparrow*. But don't understand. He doesn't see Tucker. Is He even watching what's happening? I throw another stone. Daring God to come down here and tell me to my face why He's letting this happen.

I do this until I'm spent. My skin is sticky and my dress clings. I sink to the ground, caring not for the dirt, only for the hoarseness of my throat and how horrible I feel. I sit there until the air dims. I need to be getting home, but I can't move from this spot until I know that God's heard me.

And that's the moment that I realize what I want in this life. I want to be a wife. I once envisioned it as such a simple occupation. Something very expected. I never craved it before...but I do now. My whole heart cries out for it with every ounce of conviction that Tucker's been trying to draw out of me.

But now it's the one thing I may never be because I only want to be Tucker's.

Just as another sob rises up inside me, a little flutter passes by my right shoulder. Next thing I know, a bird is landing on the path in front of me. It's a small brown bird. Maybe it's a sparrow, but I don't think it is. The bird hops closer and tilts its tiny head. Small eyes, like two glinting specks in the setting sun, look at me.

A little flutter of wings, and it hops closer. Then pecks at my shoe. My first instinct is to pull my foot away, but I make myself be very still. It hops up my laced boot onto my knee, and I know my eyes have to be as big as saucers. Another tip of its head, then just like that, it's off—flying toward the woods, its wings no more than an amber flash in the failing light.

Stiff and exhausted, I rise slowly. Home calls to me even as the sky grays, but I can't look away from the edge of the woods where that little bird vanished. Because

God's listening.

And if He sees that tiny bird, then He sees me.

More importantly…He sees Tucker.

Ma doesn't make me go to school Friday either. I am more grateful than I can say. After chores, starting in on the novel proves pointless, so I go through my box of drawing supplies—stubby pencils that have teeth marks and long, new ones that haven't even been sharpened. I grab a few new ones and the pad of paper I got for Christmas. I try not to use it often, drawing instead on my slate or scraps of paper, but today I want the best.

I eat dinner at noon but have no recollection what it was as I start down the lane again, one hand clutching my drawing pad, the other a basket of things for Tucker. Thinking of how his pa had to turn me away yesterday, I shove all worry to the wind and simply hum a song beneath the June sky.

This calmness only lasts until his dirt drive. At that point, I stride toward his house, determined to bust down the door if need be. But his ma answers my knock, and with a bittersweet smile, she ushers me in.

"Tucker's upstairs. He's not feelin' too well."

"Oh." It's all I can muster after her declaration.

She eyes my sketch pad and then the basket which I fear she might offer to take up to him. "You can go ahead on up." Her smile is sincere. "His door's open...it's the second on the left. He'll be glad to see you."

"Thank you."

She shows me to the foot of the stairs and I take quiet steps, hoping not to disturb Tucker or anyone else. It's strange to be walking up his stairs, toward his bedroom.

I peek into his open doorway and see him. He's leaning back against a mound of pillows, an arm draped behind his head, his box of slides open on his chest. A few amber bottles of medicine rest on his bedside table. He's wearing a striped nightshirt. His head shifts and he spots me but doesn't speak.

Doesn't say my name, and he doesn't smile.

All I can think about is how he'd rather be outside.

He just peers at me, and although his face is a little thinner, the faint tint beneath his eyes more pronounced, he's so handsome that it hurts.

It's the moment I realize that everything is changing. He's not going to try and keep me brave. It's now I who will be brave for him.

I muster every bit of courage I have. Force every rising tear away and grin at him. Then I march over to his bed, and though it kills me, plop down the basket and paper and simply say, "So I brought cookies. I hope you're hungry because there's a lot. I also brought a game. Do you like Parcheesi? I'm very good at it and I've been lookin' forward to finding something that I'm better at than you."

It's the last thing in the world I want to say to him. But the prayer in my heart is answered when he smiles back. It's shadowed. But I'll take it.

He chuckles a little and I poke about in the basket. Closing the box of slides, he hands it to me and I lay it aside for him. I hold up the tin I brought and set it open on the bedside table next to his microscope. "Oatmeal raisin. I think I put in too much brown sugar, but there could be worse things in life, right?" It's getting easier to pretend that nothing's wrong, and with his amused eyes roaming over me, I keep at it.

After pulling a chair over to the side of his bed, I lift two novels out of the basket and cite the titles. "If you want me to read to you, I can do all the characters' voices."

"See, now that's something you're better at than me." Slowly, he reaches over and takes a cookie. Breaking it in half, he takes a small bite. The rest vanishes beside the folds of his blanket. "I'm glad you're here," he finally says.

"Me too." I adjust my pad of paper and pencils and set them on the foot of the bed.

"Would you mind opening the window?" he asks while I'm standing near it.

I move to do it and the breeze floats in. His exhale is slow and deep. Wanting to distract him from all that he might be missing, I turn in a slow circle. "You have a very nice room." I don't have a room. Just a bunk to share with Betsy in a corner of our cabin. Maggie sleeps above us. I've never told Tucker this. "Are all of these yours?" I peek at a collection of pocket knives and glimpse wooden skis leaning in the corner.

"Yeah."

The room has a clean, pleasant smell, like freshly-washed linens and lemon wood oil. We talk for a while and Tucker tells me about some of the things he has. Things he's collected. About this time I ask if I can draw his picture, and he seems pleased.

"Make me look good, huh?"

"You'll look perfect." But I do draw him partly the way I remember him and partly the way he is now. And I realize how much I love everything about him. His ears that aren't quite the right shape. The soft bruising beneath his eyes. Some might think it a flaw, just a sign of his sickness, but it's been there as long as I've known him, and to me, it's just Tucker. So I draw it all.

I tell him he doesn't have to worry about holding too still, and he keeps adjusting himself for comfort. We talk and talk and talk.

A few final strokes and I smudge a bit of the shadows that I've come to know and love.

"Do I look presidential?" he asks when I'm too silent in concentration.

I peer at him over the tall book that's propped up in my lap. "*Very.*" I show him and he seems pleased, though he does point to his hair.

"You could've done something about that."

"I like it."

His ma comes in then with a tray that's holding steaming tin cups. It seems to be tea. It's a warm day, but Tucker looks relieved by her offering when she hands him one.

She gives me one as well and I take it. "Thank you,

Mrs. O'Shay."

There's a smile in her eyes when I take a small sip as Tucker does.

She cups the back of my head tenderly. The gesture touches me. Even so, I fear being in her way. I'm taking a piece of the precious time she has left with her son, but she just steps toward the door and gives me a kind nod. I can see in her face that she's happy he has a friend. That he's not alone.

"This is very tasty." I sip the tea again when she leaves. This feels silly to say, but it's keeping me going. Before I can dwell on anything else, he takes my hand, holding it easily. I ask Tucker if he's up for a game of Parcheesi. He says he is.

I clear the bedside table, moving his microscope and slides carefully to the bookshelf. With our mugs of tea nudged aside, I spread out the mat and wooden pawns. A few buttons of his nightshirt are undone down to his sternum. He once complimented me on my skin. While I think he was only teasing, I could very well speak the same words to him. It's *so* fetching. A warm, buttermilk color. He shifts to his side so he can reach the board, tucking his blankets around his waist. He doesn't seem discomforted for me to see him this way and I'm glad.

If only he knew how precious he is to me. The words slip out. I can't help it.

He gives me a half grin. "You're not so bad yourself." His hand finds mine again and he holds it while we play a few rounds. His skin begins to warm again.

Then it hits me. "When did you stop wearing your gloves?"

After rolling the dice, he moves a pawn. His eyes find mine over the mat of game pieces. "About the time you started holding my hand."

ELEVEN

Tucker told me that I could come back whenever I wanted on Saturday, so after a few bites of breakfast and a handful of chores, I promise Ma I'll be back before dark as I grab a fresh basket of things and pound down the front porch steps.

I'm panting by the time I pound back up Tucker's. Through the open doorway, I spot Mrs. O'Shay at the table, scooping dried beans from a sack. I shouldn't have just run up so loudly, but I forgot myself in my eagerness to be here.

Her hands still when she sees me. She blinks a few times and my heart hovers somewhere between breaking and beating, and I forget how to move.

But then she speaks. "He'll be glad to see you."

Relief rushes out in a breath.

I follow her slowly up the stairs.

Tucker's door is slightly ajar and she knocks softly,

then nudges it open. She doesn't go in. She just stands there a moment, and the sun filling his room is bright on her too. Her smile is soft and her eyes glassy when she pulls her gaze to me. Her hand cups my cheek. "I'm so thankful for you," she whispers.

My eyes sting even before she starts back down the hall.

Just a few steps and I round his doorway, seeing him. He's propped up again and his head shifts in my direction. But unlike yesterday—his face lights up. Maybe not the way it once would have, but there's an unmistakable happiness there.

Though everything inside me is tearing to pieces, I vow here and now that he will not see me cry. I edge around the door and step to his bed.

He smiles again and I touch his cheek. It's rough. I realize that he shaves every day. How did I not think of this before? I realize there are so many things that I don't know about him, and there won't be time to find them all out.

"So I have some good news," I say as cheerily as I can.

His blue eyes don't leave my face.

"I'm going to take the college entrance exams next

year. I probably won't get in and probably can't afford to go, but I'm going to try."

That endearing *V* eclipses his brows as they tip up in the middle. "Yeah?" he asks, but there's so much more in that single word. And I can see how pleased he is.

"They taught Latin and Greek at my last school, but I wasn't very good at it and am even rustier now. That's going to be my greatest hurdle. Now that I'm not so terrible at algebra, thanks to you."

The side of his mouth lifts in a smile.

"I have books for Latin and Greek. You can borrow them." He says it as if I can give them back, and despite every resolve I have, everything inside me crumbles.

My chin wobbles and my vision blurs. Within seconds, I have to swipe my sleeve over my eyes.

Tucker says my name and I look at him. He's crying too. Not like I am, but his eyes are wet. He moves his hand to the edge of the bed and I kneel there so I can hold it.

"Please don't be sad, Sarah."

I press my forehead to the blankets and fight the burn as best I can, but it's welling fiercely and more tears slip down. This is all wrong. Everything I'm doing is wrong. I'm supposed to be strong and cheerful and make him forget all that's happening. I'm not supposed to be falling to pieces right here in front of him. It's only going to make this that much worse for him.

He kisses the top of my head and I whisper, "Thank you for letting me borrow your books."

When I finally look up again, his fingers push back a bit of hair at my forehead. He studies the same spot as he speaks. "Try to take care of them, huh?" He wets his lips. "Don't lose them. And…" His damp eyes search my face. "Don't get lost yourself." His fingers are still playing with my hair. Sliding down the length of it now. "Take care of yourself…*and be happy.*"

A tear plunges, followed by another. "I don't want to be happy without you."

He smiles a little…and I can see it…the impish light in his face. The boy who got me in trouble that first day. "Well, you're just gonna have to try." He wraps a bit of my hair around his fingers. It unwinds and he begins again. I can see how tired he is.

I rest my hand on his mattress and set my chin on top so I can just watch his face. He asks me what I did today, so I tell him. It doesn't seem exciting, but his eyes close and he looks peaceful as he listens. I prattle on, trying to make it all sound as interesting as possible. His breathing grows slower and slower. I don't think he's asleep. He keeps swallowing and clearing his throat.

"Tucker?" I ask, desperately needing the sound of his voice.

"Yeah?"

"Would it…would it be all right…if I loved you forever?"

The side of his mouth lifts a little, and he squints at me as he whispers, "If you'd like."

And I want to bottle that expression. The awe there—that he's trying so hard to hide. I want to bottle the sound of his voice. His laugh and his smile.

The breeze tosses the curtains into the room, then pulls them around the windowsill, unable to make up its mind what it wants to do.

"Sarah?"

"Yeah?"

"Thank you."

I sit there for a long while. For how long, I don't know. I can't even remember how many hours are in a day. Tucker sleeps a little. He wakes in between. We talk when he does and it's so, so sweet. The day passes and I decide that, just like his mother, every moment is my favorite.

His ma comes in and brings him toast and tea as the sun sweeps low over the meadow. To my surprise, Tucker sits up a little and eats some. His cheeks color and I see a new strength in his eyes. She also mixes him up a glass of medicine which he downs with a grimace. It seems to help because within minutes, he's talking a little more.

"Will you do one more thing for me?" he asks as he breaks off another small piece of toast.

I nod.

"Just…I mean…" He sets the toast back down. "Will you forgive me?"

"Forgive you?"

"For…" He shifts his legs, wincing a little less as he does, and I can practically see the medicine working. "For not…" His hand slips from mine long enough to adjust himself. He takes mine back up in his own, holding it gently. "For earlier…when you said you loved me…"

I bite my lip to keep it from trembling.

"I should have said it back. You just…you took me by such surprise." There's that easy smile again, the one that's full of life. "I've been wanting to tell you that a hundred times, but I didn't want to make any of this worse for you. Would you mind…" His blue eyes are vulnerable as they skim my face. "Would it be all right if I told you now?"

I nod with my whole heart.

And he does.

I've never seen such joy in someone's face as what's living in his right now. As if everything is suddenly right with the world. That all is as it should be. I take his words—*I love you*—that he just whispered into my ear and hold them tightly as I watch him settle against his pillows.

He's quiet for a few minutes and I don't mind. He's just looking at me and I'm looking at him, and never has the silence held so much.

After a little while, he speaks. "I've realized something." He coughs into his hand and winces. "God didn't make a mistake with me."

I squeeze his hand tighter.

His other hand grips the blankets, working a patch with countless thoughts. "This isn't about all life...or all death. It's not one or the other." He tugs at a thread, pulling it over and over as he stares at it. Then he glances to me. "It's about living what you can live for. What God gives you the time to do. He gave me...he gave me the time to know you. To love you."

I have to swipe my face against my shoulder just to

see him properly.

"And it's these very things that once made me angry." He slides me a look that's rimmed in yearning—for me to grasp his words. "I often thought—why is God taking you away from me?" His voice grows hoarse. "Then I realized that He's still giving." Pausing, Tucker glances at his water glass, and I move to help him take a sip. I can feel his gratitude as he settles back again. "He's giving me today."

Those words press into me and I'm amazed by this young man in front of me.

"And even this moment. Sometimes that's all we have—a moment. But..." He swallows again. "It doesn't make it less." I help him take another sip. His gaze is on me as he finishes. "It just makes it more."

With the cup back on the nightstand, I resume my position—kneeling on the floor beside his bed. He shifts his head against his mound of pillows and peers up at the ceiling. He's quiet for a long while, adjusting his legs now and again. Resolution settles into his expression, and he finally speaks. "People have died for much more noble things than this." Slowly, he shakes his head, still looking up. "That used to bother me. I could have been a hero—I could have gone out saving someone, or fighting for others…but I just got *gypped*." He faces me, and it's a look that goes straight into me. "I spent a lot of time being angry at God about that." Voice soft, he nudges his chin down so his face is closer to mine. "I was sitting there being angry at God when you walked in school that day and sat beside me."

I can't stop my hand from reaching up for the side of his face. He turns into it, closing his eyes briefly.

"And what I once thought was just a cruel and dirty trick…was really a lifeline." There are his fingers again, drawing down the length of my hair where it drapes over my shoulder.

I need to tell him what a hero he is.

"Tucker," I whisper. "You are so many things to so many people. Do you know this?"

He smiles a little—a mixture of joy and sadness.

"You teach people things. And not just schooling. You taught me about kindness…and friendship," I say, wishing I could do him justice. "And you remind me to be brave. You teach me that this world is a better place than I ever realized. But also…" I pause when his forehead wrinkles as if in surprise. "You've been teaching me not to hold on too tightly to this place." I don't think he meant to teach me this, but he's doing it right now. "This isn't a place I'd have let go of easily, but I'm starting to see it now for what it is—a home to love others while we can."

He gives me that endearing look—the one where his mouth tips up on one side, brow furrowed, so childlike and wondering. So fetching that all I want to do is kiss him. Rising a little, I do just that. It's small…

But it doesn't feel small.

He's smiling when I sink back down to my knees.

The wind tugs at the curtain again and he speaks. "This…" His chest heaves a bit and I can see him growing a little breathless. "This…dying 'young and handsome' business…"

Have I told him how much I hate his humor?

"I'm not as scared about it as I once was. Granted…" He tips a shoulder in a faint, roguish shrug. "I'm not exactly…*over the moon* about it."

I brush my face against his arm to hide my smile— and my tears.

"But the thing with lying here…is it gives you a lot of time to think." Sinking down a bit, he settles lower into his pillows. "I realize that I was still mad about the injustice of it all."

I rub my forehead against his skin, savoring the feel of it.

"I was trying not to be, but I was all the same. And now, I don't know…"

His pause lifts my gaze to his face, and now I'm seeing nothing other than the eyes that I love. The ones I want to look into always. The moist blue ones that are peering down at me now.

"I try to think of good things." He wets his lip and I see my math tutor afresh. How I adore this side of him. "For example…since I *won't* be going to college—I thought I'm just going to have to find another way to keep being smarter than you."

This time I don't even try to hide my smile.

"I've started a list of questions to ask God when I get there." He swallows hard, and when he coughs a bit, I offer him another sip of water. He takes it, not so much as lifting his head from the pillow. My hand shakes as I set the cup down.

Softly, Tucker continues. "The list keeps getting longer and longer, and it's giving me something to look forward to, I suppose."

My throat is so tight I have to whisper the words. "What are you going to ask Him?"

"Well, for one…" He tugs at the thread a few times. "I want to know how He defeated the grave." Though

Tucker has sunk his head deeper into the pillows, his mouth lifts in a bittersweet smile. Then his lashes rise toward the ceiling, and his expression grows serious, voice so very soft. "And for two...I want to know how heavy the cross was to carry."

Tears burn. "I want to know those ones, too."

"Do you?" His head shifts so he can look at me.

To my surprise, his eyes are alight. I nod. Fiercely.

"Then I'll save those two for when you get there." His voice is gentle. "We'll ask Him together."

I press my face into his wrist again and make myself breathe. "It's a deal."

He kisses my hair.

Dusk is coming and it's getting late. I shouldn't walk home alone in the dark and I think he knows it too when he squeezes my hand.

"You should probably start for home," he says.

"Maybe in a few more minutes."

My arm is folded on the edge of his bed, and I rest my chin there again. My other hand is between each of his, tucked snug beneath his blankets where we're both warm. I stare at that funny little flip in the front of his hair. The one that will never lie down. I play with it some and he closes his eyes again.

"Would you like me to sing you a song?" I ask, knowing it's time for him to fall asleep again.

"Would you?"

Always.

O Holy Night comes to mind again. He wanted a Christmas song last time, so I sing this one again. But this time, when I get to the part about falling on your knees, there's no sound left to my voice at all. He's asleep. I know it because I say his name and he doesn't answer.

"I'll see you soon," I whisper as his chest slowly rises and falls.

His room is getting dark, and knowing that I can't stay here forever—no matter how badly I want to—I make myself stand. I haven't moved much in the last few hours so it isn't easy. But what *is* easy is bending down, pressing a kiss to that rough, perfect cheek, and whispering that I love him. That he's the best friend I ever had, and that I…Sarah Miller…am the luckiest girl in the whole, wide world.

TWELVE

Tucker didn't wake up the next morning. I knew because Benjamin came to tell me. I had been getting ready for church, trying to straighten the hem of my skirt one moment, and the next—I was on the ground, in the dirt, wailing Tucker's name.

Benjamin held me.

I didn't know anything could hurt that bad. I miss him terribly.

After Tucker's funeral, I climbed to the top of the hill behind my house where I didn't have to see any more people dressed in black. Wanting to do the unexpected for Tucker, I wore a gray dress, because this wasn't goodbye. Black is for goodbyes.

This was just *see you soon*.

The sound of the cavalry had faded some, so it was just me and a quiet sky. I tilted my face toward the warmth and whispered those words, hoping he heard.

Sometimes pain is kind of like love. It's just turned inside out. That's what makes it hurt so fiercely. It doesn't mean that it's bad, and as much as we want to wish it away, it may still come. And when it does, it only means that what's living on the other end of it was loved.

Greatly.

EPILOGUE

Rocky Knob, Virginia
1903

"I always wondered why you had taken that college exam," Maggie says.

We're sitting at the table in my cabin. It's not much, but it's home. My own home.

"It was a promise I had to keep." I smile, remembering the time I had tried—and completely failed—to get into Brown.

"Did you tell me this story to try and change my mind about you?" she asks.

"No." I fight the urge to confess that I didn't tell her the *whole* story. "I said all that because it was the truth. It's what happened." I look at my older sister. Maggie can be a bit cynical at times. I know she means well. She's trying.

"I just don't see how you can say that you're fine," she says. "All alone…"

"But I *am* fine." I rise and fetch the teapot to fill our cups. "I'm better than fine." I peek at her over my shoulder and my braid flips against my back. I give her a sly smile. "Weren't you listening?" My feet are bare and my nightgown brushes against them. Maggie is in her nightgown, too. Little Charlotte, my niece, lies asleep on the bed.

Maggie sighs and dabs at her eyes with her sleeve. She's been crying, and I don't blame her because I have been too. "But you were so sad." She looks at me and I know that she knows, more than anyone, how sad I was. She heard me crying each night for months.

"I was," I say, as that ache rises again. "And I'm still sad sometimes. But I'm also happy. There was too much goodness to not be happy."

Slowly, she shakes her head. "How come you never told me all this before? I thought you two were barely friends." She blinks as if trying to pull the past near, recall it clearer.

I give a small shrug. "I meant to, I suppose. But it was all hard. And you were busy with your own life." Getting married…

Maggie nibbles her lip. "I'm glad you told me. That you got it off your chest. It's quite a story." She shoots out a breath and her dark hair flutters. "Maybe—does that mean you're ready to move on?"

I pluck up a few pieces of sweet, popped corn to eat.

"There *are* plenty of eligible men around here."

I talk around the caramel corn in my mouth, which sounds ridiculous. "Move on?"

Maggie chuckles. She brought the sticky treat. When she had time to make it, I don't know, but I'm awful glad she's here. We don't get to visit often. But at least twice a year, Sarah Miller fakes one of her famous headaches that can only be cured by her sister's comfort for at least a day or two. I can always imagine Joel Sawyer, Maggie's husband, rolling his eyes when she tells him I'm ailing again. Especially as she's whipping up a batch of her caramel corn.

"That new carpenter," Maggie says, chomping on a few kernels. "The one by Saddler's Pond...he was lookin' atcha in church. You'd make a wonderful wife. And I've always envisioned you as a mother."

The little sting comes—the one that arrives whenever I think of that dream, so I tuck it safely out of sight lest the longing show. "At me? The one who smells like horse blankets?"

Maggie giggles because I'm right. There's a reason he's still available.

I pass the full-length mirror that tilts back on its stand, and in my nightgown, prop my hand on my hip and strike a subtle pose which is easy since those curves finally arrived. Still looking at my reflection, I pucker my lips.

For thirty-four, I'd say it's not bad.

"You stopped him dead in his tracks, you know," Maggie adds. "Perhaps you should say hello to him. Perhaps he'll take you for a drive."

Still peering in the mirror, I fluff my hair a bit just so I don't have to look at her. "*Perhaps* I'll stop you right there and we can change the course of this conversation."

"Sarah. You have to consider it."

People have been telling me this for years.

For years, I've had men asking why I won't go for a drive with them, or with one particularly persistent banker, why I slapped him when he cornered me in his buggy with his hot breath on my neck and his bulging vest buttons about to pop off and hit me in the face.

Do they not realize?

Do they not know?

That there was a boy who changed my life. He changed my heart and the way I saw myself and the way I saw this world. He showed me that life was beautiful whether you ran full force ahead...or walked slowly. Not to mention he could conjugate Latin verbs so well, I needed a fan. That's not something that a pail of fried chicken and attempted necking at the county fair could fix. Yes, I slapped that one too.

So they stopped asking, and I'm glad.

Besides, I still dream of Tucker. If I were a married woman, that just wouldn't feel right. So I'll keep my dreams and they can keep their buggy rides.

With Maggie fixing up her tea, I go over to my hope chest. Kneeling down, I lift the heavy lid and smell the cedar memories. Brushing aside a few odds and ends, I find the wooden box I'm looking for. Opening that, I gently move aside the folded picture that I drew of him and remember the half-dozen envelopes that were all so carefully opened by his ma. She had sat me down on their front porch a few weeks after his funeral to show me— letters from colleges. Just for Tucker.

The way she explained it, somehow Tucker's scores leaked to other universities. I don't know if that was due to Mr. Davis, but I have a hunch it was—because his eyes twinkled when I told him. It turned out that Tucker got into Brown. They offered to pay his way. There were letters from Yale and Harvard and Perelman as well.

All asking him to come.

His mother draped an arm around me, and I draped one around her. Though we cried, we laughed, too. *Our* Tucker.

We were so proud.

I told her then about all the questions he was planning on asking God, and she told me that she found his list and that it was *a mile long*. There were two questions at the top, marked with my name. I smiled through the tears.

Still kneeling at the hope chest, I tug out a blue, wool sweater. I know these are where you're supposed to put linens and all kinds of pretty things for your wedding. Maybe I ended up using mine all wrong, but I don't care. It's my chest.

Maggie watches me cross over to the bed and fold the sweater in my lap before pulling up my bare ankles. She used her chest a little differently. All the things a girl ought to have, she did, but she married a man that has made her life very difficult. I can see it by the faint bruises on her arm each time she reaches out for another handful of caramel corn.

Betsy's all grown now and married, too. She fell in love with a man who works for the railroad and now lives in Connecticut. We can tell from her letters that she has a happy life. I look over at Maggie who's only a few years older than I am. But gray brushes her hair at the temples and she has lines around her mouth that tell of sorrow.

I want to go to her husband and hit him with a shovel.

But Tucker would have just told me that I was doing the first thing that popped into my head again, and he would have been right.

So instead, I live here. Just a stone's throw away. A place for my sister to come when she needs to. A place my nieces often visited. Lonnie's gone away now. Addie too. I can still remember when Lonnie was born. I was nearly eighteen and that little baby girl with the big, brown eyes was the light of my life. She still is. All grown up with a husband of her own, she lives with Addie and some good folks who had kept the girls safe. I'm so happy about this, but I miss them terribly. So much so that I remind my sister that I'm planning a visit and will be leaving in a week. I've been asking Maggie to come with me. She always promises to think about it, and I can see in her eyes how much she wants to see her daughters.

Maybe I should just hit Joel with a shovel anyway and she can make her escape.

Maggie must interpret my staring silence as something else. She pins me with one of her famous looks—soft but direct. "Did you ever tell her? Lonnie?"

"No." I never told my niece about that time, about Tucker. But I wish I had. I'm going to tell her when I see her. One of the reasons I'm more eager to go than ever.

Charlotte stirs a little in her sleep, but she's just turning over. I rise to snuggle the blanket up closer around her shoulders and give her little three-year-old cheek a kiss. Beside her on the nightstand is my Bible where the card is pressed between the Psalms, reminding me daily that *His eye is on the sparrow*.

It truly is. I've felt it every day.

I settle back on the edge of my bed and unfold the sweater. Its navy blue and I try not to wear it often, that way I won't have to wash it often and wear it out, but every now and again…

I slide my wrists into the sleeves that are too long until they poke through, then pull the rest over my head, covering me in my nightgown. I'm so glad his ma let me have this. She's gone now, but I've stayed close with

Tucker's family.

His sister and I visit regularly. She and her husband check in on me more than they should to make sure I don't need anything. Last week, before I even poured her coffee, Mary told me that Benjamin's wife had passed away and that they had a quiet service. It was announced at church the following day. Heartbroken, I knew I needed to do something. Benjamin loved Violet so. And like me, he mourned Tucker fiercely.

Benjamin had always been a bit quiet around me after that day in the yard, and I never quite knew what to say to him. We just shared a few sad smiles now and again at church. Especially the snowy mornings I woke up to find that my woodpile had grown taller in the night.

Yesterday I brought him cookies.

He thanked me as I set the tin on the banister, then he tilted his face toward the ground. I saw in his silence how much he was hurting as he slipped his hands into his pockets. Those hands—and corded forearms—the very ones that lifted our hearts to his shoulder to be carried across the churchyard that day with his pa and two other men. An act of love and loss that he had likely just done again.

Wanting to help, I played with the young ones in the

yard while he sat on the porch, watching. It was just a quiet game. I sang a little, too. The children seemed to like that.

Violet had always let me hold her babies, so each of their names comes easy. I know their eyes and their smiles. Even as I sat cuddling close the little ones, I made a vow to bring another tin of cookies. Benjamin took a maple cream for himself, so I'll make those again.

I'll throw in some shortbread as well. Tucker's favorite. Ankles pulled up on the mattress, I hold them and smile at my sister. "Did I mention the first time he kissed me?"

"No. You seem to have left that part out." She gapes at me in that sisterly way, as if she's unable to believe how I could have not disclosed such a detail. Sisters are very good at that, though.

I grin at her, and feeling her scrutiny much too much, rise to fetch my recipe box.

"*And…*" she practically sings it, trying to help me along.

"Well…I mean no wrong toward 'Mr. Carpenter near Saddler's Pond'"— or any of those other pushy suitors, for that matter. I pause long enough to pull the recipe for maple creams from the little box. "But there's no way one of those fellas can kiss like that."

And suddenly I'm sixteen again. Tucker's calling my name...trying to run after me. I was crying because I remember wiping my sleeve over my eyes. I can still recall the feel of his fingers in my hair. His mouth against mine. His warmth and his life. The sound of the cavalry. Trumpets and drums so loud that they hurt my ears.

I'm so glad that I turned back. I'm so glad that I had to sit beside him that day in school. That I ate lunch with him. I'm glad that I was terrible at algebra and I'm glad that he could kiss so well—be so wonderful and beautiful and kind—that it made my knees buckle.

It was him.

It was *always* him. And it's still him.

I've grown much too quiet because Maggie pitches a piece of caramel corn at me. "That good, huh?"

I grin and throw a piece back. "*That* good." I still don't think my feet have hit the ground yet.

NOTE TO READERS

Tucker O'Shay is the first character I've ever written who has woken me up in the middle of the night and made me press my hand to the center of my chest, just to try to rub away the ache. Sometimes, I even cried. If you're like me, you may have a few crumpled tissues beside you or a damp sleeve. How I wish I could reach out and give you a big, big hug. Know that I'm doing it in my heart. Thank you, friends, for taking this journey with me and Sarah and Tucker, and being willing to open your heart to a young man who had so much life left to live, love left to give—and gave it the best ways he could, making him a *hero* through and through.

I hope that this story is an encouragement to you. A gentle reminder that, as we face seasons in life, whether laced with joy or heartache, we can cling to truth and hope. To see the chapter of our lives that we are in—and seek the blessings God has placed there for us.

Each book I write teaches me something different. This

book has taught me to be braver. All because of Tucker—who he was—what he demonstrated in life. I confess there were many days that I didn't think I should write a story with a hero *like* Tucker. But as I began to write and he wanted Sarah to think a little more outside the box, it challenged me to do the same. A romance with a young man like Tucker in the center of it? It didn't seem possible. It didn't seem like a story that anyone would want to read. But for all the Sarahs and Tuckers out there, I had to be brave enough to try. Thank you for walking this journey as well. My prayer is that this story might have blessed you as you've blessed me.

READER'S GUIDE

1. How are Tucker and Sarah different from one another? In what ways do they complete each other and spur one another on? Who in your life has been that to you?

2. In the beginning of the story when Sarah decides to go sit by Tucker during the lunch hour, she decides that life is short and that if she doesn't go, she may always regret it. What would you have done in her situation? Have there been instances in your life when you experienced a similar crossroad?

3. What do you think of Tucker's aspirations for the future? Why do you think he dreams big? And why do you think he's holding on to those despite all that he's facing?

4. In order to be accepted into most universities in the late 1800s, students were required to take entrance exams that often spanned three major disciplines: classical languages such as Latin and Greek, history, and advanced mathematics—

without the use of calculators. In addition, they were often tested on written compositions and geography. If you were able to study in these disciplines, do you feel that you would have gotten into college during the 1800s? If not, where do you think life might have taken you?

5. Few people in Tucker's life ever loved him as much as his brother Benjamin. In what ways did you see Benjamin's admiration and respect for Tucker shine through? What kind of impact might those moments have had on Tucker? On Sarah?

6. How did knowing Tucker change Sarah as a teenage girl? How about in the years that followed?

7. How did knowing Sarah change the time that Tucker had left on this earth?

8. If you've read the Cadence of Grace series, you may have seen some characters you recognized. What do you think of them in their early years? How did life change them?

9. At the end of the story, Sarah describes the pain she feels as being a lot like love—it's just turned inside out. Have there been times in your life where you've felt this? What got you through?

10. What do you think might lie on the horizon for Sarah?

11. Looking around at your own life, who do you see that might need a bit of encouragement? Whether it's a hug, or a card, or simply them knowing that you see them…how might you be able to reach out and comfort a neighbor or friend?

ACKNOWLEDGMENTS

Though the novella itself may be small, the army behind it is mighty. Thank you to my early readers: Cathy Davis, for your nursing expertise; and Amanda Dykes, Beverly Nault, and Rachelle Rea for providing content edits galore. And to my mom for being my first-ever reader, even in the late hours of the night! To Meghan Gorecki and my darling teen beta-readers, the Gaggle of Giggles–Hadassah Manchester, Kezia Manchester, and Kara Swanson. You all made this so much fun! To Denise Harmer, for being an amazing copy editor; and to Andrea Cox, for your proofing skills—you both blessed me so much. And a great big thanks to Lynnette Bonner, for so generously helping me navigate Photoshop from the other side of the country. And to Gail Shalan for an amazing performance for the audio version. Thank you for bringing Tucker and Sarah's story to life! A very special thanks to the beautiful team of endorsers for *This Quiet Sky*–Katie Ganshert, Beth K. Vogt, Karen Cecil Smith, Rissi Cain, Kristy Cambron, and Heather Day Gilbert. Thank you also goes to my agent, Sandra Bishop, for steadily walking this road with me. You are a gem.

Christy Award-finalist and author of *Be Still My Soul, Though My Heart is Torn*, and *My Hope is Found*, **Joanne Bischof** has a deep passion for Appalachian culture and writing stories that shine light on God's grace and goodness. She lives in the mountains of Southern California with her husband and their three children. You can visit her website at www.joannebischof.com.

MORE FROM

JOANNE BISCHOF

Gideon only ever cared about himself.
Now that Lonnie is his wife,
will he ever be worthy of her heart?

BOOK ONE IN THE

- CADENCE OF GRACE -

SERIES

TO HEAR

THIS QUIET SKY

-PERFORMED-

Available through Amazon

and Audible

CPSIA information can be obtained at www.ICGtesting.com
Printed in the USA
LVOW04s0035161015

458413LV00026B/557/P